# Ringstones

Black Curtain Press
PO Box 632
Floyd VA 24091

ISBN 13: 978-1627553605


First Edition
10 9 8 7 6 5 4 3 2 1

# Ringstones

## Sarban

# Part One

The Reason why I, and not Piers Debourg, have undertaken to write the introduction and conclusion to Daphne Hazel's story is that I possess a typewriter and Piers Debourg does not At least, that is the reason Piers gave for not doing it and it seemed cogent until the ache in my shoulder-blades made me examine his argument more critically. The real reason, I now suspect, is that if I had not done it, neither of the other two would, and I was sufficiently interested to want to see the story properly finished off, though insufficiently experienced to foresee the labour of it and, in fact, the impossibility of it. I discovered too late that I could not write the conclusion of the story; but still, I have for my pains a copy of Daphne Hazel's manuscript (Piers has kept the original) and the rest may pass as annotations of the text.

I had arranged by letter to spend the last few weeks of the Long Vacation in Northumberland or walking on the Border with Piers Debourg. He met me at the station and we went up to his suburb on the trolley-bus.

As we turned into Northumberland Street the broad sunlight blazed on the gilt of the only landmark I have in Newcastle.

"It always seems to me," said I, "one of the more whimsical eccentricities of the English character that this black, bleak city, this soul-constricting agglomeration of granite and grime, where the people seem to have been born with overcoats on their backs and Rechabitism in their hearts, should have erected for its tutelary deity a figure of Caligulan luxury: a naked, golden girl. I can never quite believe it. Does anyone else ever see it, I wonder? And yet once, I suppose, the design for it must have been passed by a sober and completely-clothed Board of Directors. How? I wonder. Did some mad journeyman of the Northern Goldsmiths' Company cast a spell on the Board and beguile them with a dream he had of the Emperor's workshops in Byzantium? Or did some incredible, top-hatted, dundrearied Director return from an Eastern tour haunted by the image of a goddess poised in a marble portico between golden sun and violet sea there where the light wave lisps Greece? Or was it a moralist who posed her there above the clock to say to thoughtless youth, "Behold, pleasure passeth but gold endureth"?

"Or Beauty escapes from the bonds of Time," suggested Piers in a tone implying that he could fit you a moral to any fable from stock. "Hasn't it occurred to you that it might be the last wild nymph of Northumberland bagged by the Chairman after lunch on that memorable Twelfth of August in 1866?"

"I might question the strict accuracy of that 'bagged'," I said. "But there's one insuperable objection to nymphs in Northumberland, and that's your climate. If you insist on classical fauna I'll go so far as to allow you satyrs, because satyrs are comfortably accommodated with hair breeches, but I never saw a nymph that I'd call really adequately attired to stand up to your confounded nethering East wind."

"They might have been migrants," said Piers. "Summer visitors like swallows. Your objection wouldn't hold this summer. Northumberland's as hot as Arcady. In fact, why shouldn't they hibernate and only come out in exceptional summers? Wouldn't you say a sun like this might lure more than one sort of shy creature out of hiding?" He looked at me rather oddly and laughed. "That's a possible materialistic explanation which I put forward, not very seriously, to account for something curious I've got to show you."

That stopped my speculations about the golden girl, but before I could find out what was on Piers's mind we had arrived at the stop near his house. He jumped up and clattered down the steps as the trolley-bus slowed down.

The Debourgs live in a tall old house in a quiet street not far from the Town Moor. In front it looks upon a tract of allotments which once, I believe, was a public garden or a cricket pitch or something less utilitarian than it is today; while behind, the windows of the house give on to an alleycat's heaven of higgledy-piggledy rooftops, outhouses and sheds: a labyrinth of blackened bricks and mortar, looking perhaps even more dreary under the September sunshine than it did under the thick cloud and grey curtains of rain that had veiled it for the whole of my last visit in the Easter Vacation. I had penetrated that labyrinth several times, for in the heart of it is a little square surrounded by tumbledown black stone cottages which Piers declares was once the village green, and in this square stands the Admiral Benbow. But I would never attempt to steer a course to the Admiral, let alone away from him, without Piers for pilot.

We had a Northern High Tea which was protracted to something near the Southern dinner-time by cheerful conversation with Piers's mother and father; then, when Mrs. Debourg had turned down our not very insistent offer to help wash the pots, we went out and boarded the Admiral, where we found entertainment enough to delay us until supper time.

Our help in washing-up the supper things was not scorned, I remember. Or perhaps it was not noticed in time for objection to be made, for Piers's father had got fairly launched at the supper-table on tales of his boyhood in Connemara and was not to be interrupted by the mere trifles of domestic routine. So we all four moved into the kitchen and the pots were washed among us while we followed him through a long story about a joiner's apprentice, a corpse, a screwdriver, a top-hat and a stone jar of whisky.

It was late when Piers and I went upstairs, but we did not go straight to bed. We climbed a further flight to one of the little attic rooms under the roof which Piers uses as his own study. There we sat, as we have sat many an hour between a night and its morning in his rooms or mine at Christ's, smoking our pipes—I was going to say in a silence of mutual understanding, but Newcastle beer, unlike the quiescent gripe-water sold under that name in some parts of this realm, retains even in these times a certain independence of action, so the mutual understanding was not entirely silent. Still, it was inarticulate for a long time, until Piers remarked:

"You've heard me talk about Daphne Hazel?"

"I have then," I replied. "Sorry, but I always begin to pick up the Celtic idiom after listening to your father for an hour or two.

That's the weakness of your student of languages— always more attentive to the manner than the matter of a discourse. But what about her?" "She's a sane sort of person," he observed. "You mean her lucid intervals come fairly close together? Well, that's a satisfactory condition, ain't it? What's remarkable about that? Except its rarity, of course."

"You know she and I were good friends at school. We've written to each other at intervals all this last year while she's been at Towerton. She's training to be a gym-teacher. I hadn't heard from her for some time, though, until yesterday when I received a communication." "Telepathic, telegraphic, or merely postal?" "Well, written, anyway, and sent by post." "And that's shaken your faith in her sanity? Ah well Nothing's ever quite what it seems. But what are the exact grounds of certification?"

I remember that Piers took some time to reply. The little I knew about Daphne Hazel up to this time is soon told: Piers had mentioned her to me quite often in the two years I had known him. I had an impression of a lively, intelligent, level-headed girl who had taken with him a leading part in all the Sixth-Form activities at their school and been somewhat lonely when he, being a year older, went up to Cambridge and she stayed on another year at Whitehill Secondary School. I imagined that she must have been reckoned a clever girl: she seemed, from his talk, to have been as interested in books as he was; but she wanted to get out of the predestined academic grooves laid down for ninety per cent of Secondary School boys and girls who go on to the Higher School Certificate: I mean, a Training College, or a University if they're lucky, and then a job in an elementary or secondary school. She was unhappy at home: she wanted to get away and do something different and she thought she was doing it by getting a scholarship to Towerton Physical Training College. Piers obviously wished she had gone up to Cambridge.

"Oh, the oddity is slight enough," he said. "It's not so much the things she writes about as that it's she who should write about them."

That filled me with forebodings. But I know my duty when Piers begins to talk about literature.

"You mean that up to now you've assumed that she enjoyed the possession of what a plain man would call a healthy mind?"

"If you're that plain man, yes," he said. "And another thing to bear in mind is that at a place like Towerton she's not likely to have come under influences that would encourage the germination of elvish fancies and eerie illusions. I take it that a Physical Training College is the sort of place where *Mens Sana in Corpore Sano* is inscribed in letters six foot high on the hygienically tiled walls of every well-ventilated cubicle; where a day that begins at six a.m. with, a cold shower and is divided equally between the gym and the playing-field with brief intervals for wholesome, balanced meals, leaves the body so drowsed with healthy exertion that the minute it tumbles into bed its tenant mind has no option but to draw the blinds likewise and slumber in a blissful blank till cheerful morning bell peals out on the brisk air of day again."

"Christ!" I said. "It sounds like the seamy side of a concentration camp to me. Was it for this they hanged the Beast of Belsen?"

"Well, some such antiseptic odour of sanity did breathe from her letters from Towerton. True, she's only been at this temple of Freud durch Kraft for a year, and she had imagination; but it's seemed to me from her letters up to now that her powers of invention were under control. In fact, I'm much more likely to spin fairy-tales for the fun of them than she is; and yet..."

"Dammit, Piers, you're very mystifying," I said. "Stop yetting and tell me what she's written. I haven't often noticed you being perturbed by the eccentricities of your friends, and for my part I can't see why even a gym-teacher shouldn't occasionally skip up a ladder to the lordly lofts of Bedlam and come down with a straw or two in her hair. After all, they shake out."

Piers got up and opened the cupboard in the corner of the room where he keeps his papers. He brought out a stiff-backed exercise book.

"You know," he said, pausing with this in his hand, "she got a job for the Long Vac. at a place up here in Northumberland. She mentioned it to me in the last letter I had from her before their term-end. It seemed the sort of thing that would interest her and that she'd do very well: looking after some foreign kids. I was hoping I should see her up here and I was waiting to hear the address of the place so that we could fix something up. Well, she hasn't written to me since then until yesterday, when I got this."

I took the book and flicked the pages over. It was full of legible-looking handwriting.

"It's a longish thing," Piers said, "and it's getting late now. Would you like to take it and read it sometime before you get up tomorrow and tell me what you think of it?"

I feel that I weighed the duties of friendship rather ungraciously against that fat exercise book for a moment before I resigned myself to saying: "Provided you allow me to get up at my usual hour I might manage it." And on that we parted for the night.

I didn't really want to lose any sleep over Daphne Hazel's "communication". To tell the truth, I was afraid that the book threatened a lengthy exercise in self-analysis, some masterpiece of introspection no doubt absorbingly interesting to Daphne Hazel and considerably so to Piers, but not at all to me. I couldn't even exploit it for the purposes of my Tripos. I am reading Oriental Languages and should find a dissertation on the Permutations of the Infirm Letters both more instructive and more entertaining.

I fully intended, therefore, to leave the manuscript until my morning cup of tea put me in a more indulgent frame of mind. But, a document is a document, and I could not help but give a glance at it as I smoked my last pipe in bed. Alas for prudent resolution... I stayed awake until I had finished the book and that was at some hour in the morning the existence of which I am normally loath to admit.

This is as much introduction as Daphne Hazel's story needs, and here it follows, faithfully typed out by my own two forefingers.

# Daphne Hazels Story

One evening shortly before the end of last term three or four of us, all Juniors, were having coffee in Miss Corrigan's room, as we usually do two or three nights a week. Miss Corrigan lectures on Anatomy, Biology, the Chemistry of the Body and Dietetics. We all like her. She's unconventional and when she lectures there's some fun in even a dry subject like chemistry. There is a standing invitation to Juniors and Seniors alike to have coffee in her room after dinner and our particular gang have acquired the habit of using her room almost as a common-room, or, as she tells us, a nursery.

I remember the people who were there that evening. There was Connie Webster, Mu. Jordan, Teresa Faldingworth, Mary Paxton and myself. We had finished the First Year Exams that day and were in a mood of hilarious relief. We were noisy and inclined to throw ourselves about all over the place. We quietened down after a while. Connie Webster and Mu. Jordan, I remember, had been wrestling over a photo on Corrigan's divan and they sprawled rather untidily there. The rest of us lay inelegantly but comfortably on the carpet round Corrigan's chair.

Someone began to talk about what she was going to do in the Vac. and so we came to gossip about holidays. Mu. Jordan said she had applied through the Students' Union for a holiday job in Holland. Somebody else said she wouldn't mind having a job during the Vac, and then Miss Corrigan said: "Well then, why doesn't one of you take this on?" And she fished a letter out of a stuffed paper-rack beside her chair. "It's an old acquaintance of mine," she said, "who wants someone to coach two or three foreign children during the summer holiday. It's up in Northumberland."

We asked rather indifferently what the place was like. "I can't tell you that," she said, "because I was never there. My friend's been buried these many years in archaeology, so maybe you won't be able to step across the house for folio volumes or see across it for the dust rising from them; and it's beyond conjecture what sort of little imps the foreign brats will be. But if one of you likes to take the risk there's the address." She tore off the top of the letter and dropped it into my lap—no doubt because I was the nearest.

Later I showed it round but no one was particularly interested, so I kept it by me for a few days. I did not, just then, think seriously of doing anything about it myself. As Term-end approached, however, and I heard, all round me, talk of going away to this and that exciting-sounding place, I began to wish that I had something fixed up for the holidays instead of just having to go back to Whitehill and spend all a long summer with Aunt Elizabeth and Uncle Fred. Someone asked me where I was going for my holiday and the vision I had then of Whitehill and the deadly dullness of Green Street determined me. I took out the scrap of paper again and wrote to the address it gave:


Dr Marcus Ravelin,
Beeches Hotel,
Great Russell Street,
London.


On the last day of term I received an answer. It asked if I would call on Dr Ravelin at his hotel any afternoon between four and six during the following week. I had already packed up, so I decided to go up to London at once. I took my trunk with me and left it at Waterloo Station cloakroom while I went by bus to Great Russell Street. I was a little worried about my expenses as, after paying the fare from Towerton to Waterloo, I had only £.4 10s. left out of my scholarship allowance, the next payment of which is not due until the beginning of the Autumn Term. I didn't know how much it would cost to spend a night in London: Miss Corrigan had given me the name of a hotel, but she was vague about the price. Out of my four pounds ten I had to pay my fare to Whitehill, which is two pounds twelve and fourpence.

I had been feeling rather shy of going by myself into a big London hotel, but I found that Beeches was quite a small place and the Hall Porter was very kindly. When I asked for Dr Ravelin he took me at once along a corridor and showed me into a high room furnished with old-fashioned mahogany and horse-hair furniture. A small, grey-haired man was sitting at a table on which a number of books lay open.

I saw Dr Ravelin then as a neat elderly gentleman; dapper, in an old-fashioned way. He wore what Daddy used to call a Gates-of-Heaven collar with a white-spotted blue bow tie, and a dark grey suit with all four buttons of the jacket buttoned. I thought his manner was rather formal and my nervousness wasn't helped very much by his trick of cocking his head sharply on one side and raising his bushy eyebrows at each answer I made, as if I surprised ruin. The horse-hair easy chair he invited me to sit on had been made for some kind of anatomy quite different from mine, for I slipped and slid about on it and felt anything but easy.

He questioned me about my course at Towerton, my age, hobbies, games and so on, and his questions were so much at random that I began to suspect that the business of engaging a temporary governess or coach or nursemaid or whatever I was supposed to be was something out of his line. He asked me about my family—where I lived, how long I had lived there, what other relations I had besides my Aunt and Uncle (he made no comment except "Hm!" when I told him I had none). Then about my school and my childhood until I think we had pretty well covered my complete biography.

He put the tips of his fingers together and appeared to think hard. Then he said:

"Very good, Miss Hazel, very good. Now you must want to ask me something." He cocked his head on one side, waiting.

"The children, sir," I said, not knowing at all what questions I ought to ask. "Do they speak English?"

"Some. Some. Yes, one of them speaks English quite well. Yes, you will find him quite far advanced."

"They're boys, then?" I said.

"One. One boy. Fifteen or thereabout. Yes, fifteen. You have no experience of teaching boys?"

"Well, no," I said. "But then I haven't any experience of teaching at all, except two weeks' school practice and that was simply taking little girls for gym."

"It's not important," he said. "What I envisage is not regular lessons by any means. After all, it's the summer holiday, eh?"

He smiled a rapid little smile. "What I conceive to be most useful is that the children should be encouraged to practise their English with someone capable of correcting it, and that there should be someone there to keep an eye on their general health and welfare. I am somewhat occupied myself."

"Their parents aren't with them, then?" I asked.

"No. No. As you say, their parents aren't with them. These children belong to some very old friends of mine. They like being at Ringstones. I like them to be there. But I feel now that, my habits and pursuits being what they are, I cannot really look after them without some more qualified assistance."

I privately thought my qualifications were a bit thin. I thought of Fourth Form boys at Whitehill and profoundly hoped that this foreign boy would be better-mannered and more manageable. I wondered how I ought to frame the question I wanted to ask about the pay and my board and lodging. I suppose I took so long to think it out that he thought I had finished, because he patted the tips of his fingers together and said, "Very good. Very good, Miss Hazel. I shall let you know my final decision in the morning. May I know where you are staying?"

I told him the Empire Hotel, that being the name of one that Miss Corrigan had given me. He rose and shook hands with me and I moved to the door.

As I reached it he said, quite sharply, "Miss Hazel!"

I turned round, surprised, to see him indicating the chair again.

"Miss Hazel," he said, when I had sat down again. "You may think it curious, but when I saw you walk to the door I made up my mind. A person's back, you know, can be very expressive in motion. You are quite suitable for the employment I have in mind. If you please we can settle the necessary details here and now."

I remember feeling both puzzled and amused at this; but it was rather pleasing to think that I had acquired enough of the Towerton style to impress him to that extent. So, after a few awkward hums and ha's on his part it was settled that I should begin work that day week and get £30 for the three months. I hadn't the vaguest idea whether this was much or little for the job, but it sounded a lot of money to me. Dr Ravelin wrote down the exact address for me: Ringstones Hall, Blagill, near Staineshead. My wondering whether I could borrow the money for the train and bus fare from Uncle Fred was cut short by Dr Ravelin writing me out a cheque for five pounds.

"Let me see," he said. "My reading at the British Museum will occupy me for several days more. I hope I shall be at Ringstones in time to welcome you. But in any case I will write immediately to Mrs. Sarkissian, my housekeeper, and she will have everything ready for you. I ought to tell you that Ringstones is a very quiet country place: you might even call it remote. We lack many of the amenities of town life, but I hope you won't find it uncomfortable. Whether you find it enjoyable depends on whether you can amuse yourself with outdoor activities. I think, from what you tell me, that you can." He smiled and added: "It's only fair to warn you that you'll find life with these children quite strenuous. But then, that was why I applied to Miss Corrigan to help me to find someone for them. Finally, let me persuade you not to stay at the Empire. These big places are never very comfortable. I happen to know that there is a room vacant here and you'll find Beeches a great deal more to your liking." I took his advice and was looked after very well.


## 2


My Aunt and Uncle take pleasure in asking questions and refusing to understand the answers. Back in Whitehill I encountered a weight of disapproval that left me with just the same suffocating feeling in my chest as one of my Aunt's Yorkshire puddings does. I have been away from Green Street long enough, however, to put up a better defence than I once could. I made great play with the argument, not strictly true, that the job had been found for me by the College; but the one that weighed with Uncle Fred in the end was that I should be earning money instead of spending it. (I did not tell him how much I was going to get.) In any case, I had firmly made up my mind that no amount of Green Street disapproval was going to rob me of a holiday to which I was looking forward with such excitement, I had already sent on my trunk as passenger's luggage in advance from King's Cross and, according to my promise, I set out on the Tuesday after I arrived at Whitehill and reached Ringstones Hall safe and sound that evening.

I have never been in this part of the North before. I found it very different from the country round Whitehill, and a world away from the rich meadows and woods and sleepy little rivers round about Towerton. This is a country of bleak, blunt moorland hills, black stone walls, stone cottages roofed with black slabs, wind-twisted thorns and sycamores crouching in hollows of lonely hillsides and gurgling brown peaty burns foaming like beer over black rocks in narrow and rough little glens. The very air seems wider, emptier than it does in the South, and there is a loneliness in these tracts of shaggy boggy moor such as I never knew one could feel in England before.

Ringstones lies in the very heart of the moors, in a valley whose stream is fed by the spongy bogs of all the surrounding hills. The nearest other houses are at Blagill, a little hamlet three or four miles away across the moor.

I had sent a telegram to Ringstones to say that I should arrive at Staineshead at four-twenty and take the next bus. I had some time to wait and it's quite a long way from Staineshead to Blagill by the road, so it was well on into the evening when I got down at the sharp corner of the road which the bus conductor assured me was Blagill. The few low houses lie up a glen away from the road and you do not immediately see them as you alight I walked, following the conductor's waved direction, a short way up the stony lane towards the hamlet, gazing round me with delight and a feeling of exhilaration at the high hills, so clean and fresh-looking, so free in the broad extent of their stone-walled pastures and the unfenced wastes of heather and bracken into which, near the skyline, those pastures merged.

The first thing I saw in Blagill was a pony and trap hitched to a stone gate-post. By the pony's head stood a short, dark, sulky and foreign-looking man. He touched his cap, said "Ringstones?" in a questioning way and, at my reply, took my suitcase and helped me into the trap without another word. Nor did he speak all the way to the Hall. For the first part of the journey he strode along leading the pony, for the rough lane led very steeply uphill. I had never ridden in a trap before, and the

lane was so steep and the pony plunged so suddenly and
fiercely at the rises, tilting the trap at such a sharp angle, that
I clutched the sides, afraid that I should be thrown out of the
thing, and I would have jumped out if I hadn't been more afraid
of looking silly.

After as near as I can judge a mile of this plunging progress
we twisted suddenly between two high banks tufted with heather
and here, pulling the pony momentarily to a stop, the dark man
sprang very lightly into the trap and sat on the seat beside me,
while the pony went away over the more level track at a trot.
From this point nearly all the way to Ringstones we followed a
road, or track, which, though rough enough and frequently
dipping down to fords through little streams, kept, on the whole,
to one level of moor. We seemed to branch off from the original
track and then to branch again, and in the end so twisted and
turned about round dark tarns and pallid grey-green mosses
and between miniature cliffs of peat whiskered with heather
roots that I lost all sense of direction. The long blue lines of hills
that bounded the view were so featureless that I could pick up
nothing on the skyline by which to obtain any idea of the course
we were taking.

Only one thing, or group of things, I noticed in all this tract
of moor that I thought I might stand a reasonable chance of
recognising again: that was a number of big stones, all
embroidered with grey and golden lichens, that reared up out of
the heather away on our left front and which, as we passed
within a few hundred yards of them, seemed to be situated on
a wide, low, flat mound tolerably free of heather and rising a few
feet above the shaggy surrounding waste.

Shortly after passing these things our track went downhill
and, after running between banks for some little distance,
turned sharply along the lip of a deep valley. Then I saw below
me the tops of trees and a silver glint of water in a little level
space of parkland which made an astonishing contrast with the
tangled steeps of bracken and heather and the bare grey crags
that ringed it almost completely round. In this little park, half
concealed by some very high and branching trees, stood a long,
low steep-roofed stone house of which I caught a glimpse from
the brow of the hill but which was lost to sight among the trees
before we had got far down the steep road to the park.

I did not know that it was possible to find a house so isolated and set in such unspoiled natural scenery in these days in this country. I suppose I have grown up in days and in places where angular plantations of pylons and skeins of wires strung across the sky and shiny bands of tarmac road curving over every hill are accepted as inevitable. The country round Towerton is reckoned some of the loveliest in England and yet there you are hardly ever in a spot where you can't see either an electric-power cable standard or a main road. It had occurred to me as we were crossing the moor above Blagill that all the way I was seeing nothing that a Roman centurion leading a patrol beyond the Wall would not have seen; here at the door of the Hall I thought there was nothing I could see that would not have met the eye of a straggler from Prince Charlie's army.

Mrs. Sarkissian, as I guessed her to be, met me at the door and exchanged a few words in a foreign language that I did not recognise with the man who had brought me in the trap. Her English when she spoke to me was good, and it was ordinary English, not the well-nigh incomprehensible dialect of the Staineshead people. In fact, if it had any local tinge at all, I should say it had a trace of Cockney in it.

She took me first to my room. I feel that "room" is the wrong word. It was a chamber, lacking nothing that should characterise a seventeenth century bedchamber and containing nothing, except my things, to remind me of the twentieth century. What first took my eye that evening was the huge four-poster bed such as I had seen only in pictures before, and next, the deeply-recessed mullioned window with its wide view over the park— a splendid picture of summer green and gold backed by rich browns and purples. A lattice of the window stood open, and into the bedroom came the murmuring and chuckling of ceaselessly hurrying water mingled with a whispering of leaves. As I stood there, with one knee on the broad windowseat, gazing out, there came to me such a sweet, strong freshness of evening air that I felt I could draw in a breath as deep as to my toes and still not satisfy my thirst for it.

I felt a pang of envy—of retrospective envy, as it were— for the lucky children who were spending their summer holidays there. If only I could have had a holiday in such a place when I was fifteen! Looking down at that inviting turf below and listening to that chuckling stream I felt I was going to make up for lost time.

The family's tea, Mrs. Sarkissian said, was over, but thee was something for me in her room. There, by the abrupt turns of little passages and a steep stair between walls panelled with dark oak, she led me. The "something" was a substantial tea—a boiled egg, scones, tarts, bread and jam, cake, and more butter than I've seen in one dish in my life before. It was spread on a clean scrubbed table in a wide and comfortable room with a window that looked out on to a tidy stone-flagged yard. A large smoky-blue cat was dozing on the print cushion of a wicker chair and raised a sleepy head to inspect me as I sat down. A canary hopped up and down in a cage hanging in the big window.

## 3

The climax of my pleasure that evening and the final assurance that my job was going to be a holiday came when I met the children.

While finishing my tea, and after that settling the various little pieces of domestic business to do with my ration book, my washing, shopping and so forth, I had learned from Mrs. Sarkissian that Dr Ravelin was back at Ringstones but that he would not be free until dinner. I wanted before then to have got over what I looked upon as something like the moment of receiving the question paper in an examination. The first moment, I felt, would tell me whether I could do it or not; whether my job at Ringstones was going to be a delight or a misery.

The children, Mrs. Sarkissian said, were somewhere about the house waiting to see me. She had told them they were not to bother me until I had had my tea. We went from her room through the house into the front hall. There she peeped through a door into a small sitting-room.

"That's their room," she said. "But they're not there. Wait a minute. I'll go and call them."

She went away down a passage and left me to look round

the hall. A wide oak staircase with one turn led up to a little gallery from which, it seemed, the upstairs passages led off. The banisters and rails were richly carved and turned. The hall itself was panelled nearly to the top of the walls and there were several dark old paintings hanging up, but no collections of arms or heads of animals such as I expected to see in such a house. I wondered if Dr Ravelin's predecessors had all been students like himself. By one wall was a big chest ornamented with intricate brass-work and studded all over with brass nails, and on the stone flags were several dark red rugs which I thought must be Persian. I wandered round, gazing up at the dim pictures, and finally came back to the foot of the stairs where I stood on the bottom step, leaning against the stout carved end-post of the banisters and looking across the hall, out at the brilliant picture of sunlit grass and trees framed by the half-open front door.

Suddenly there came a swift light pit-pat of feet on the stairs behind me and before I could turn round a cool hand touched me lightly on the back of the neck. There, a few steps above me, leaning down with one hand on the banister, was a young boy. He was arching his brows and looking at me with an expression that plainly said he was only waiting for me to smile to burst into delighted laughter. I smiled, and he shouted with glee.

"Nuaman?" I asked, laughing myself. He nodded and became suddenly serious, studying me with thoughtful, dark eyes. I knew, looking back at him as he steadily looked me up and down, that we were going to be good friends. I had never seen so beautiful a boy nor one whose face expressed such gaiety and at the same time such tranquillity and wisdom. There was innocence and eagerness too, I thought, in that small brown face; a kind of wonder and desire to see and learn and know. All my misgivings about teaching vanished. There could be only joy in teaching Nuaman. Because I notice such things I wondered at the perfection of his physical development. There was no awkwardness or gawkiness about him. He was dressed in a pair of little green corduroy shorts and a cream silk shirt with short sleeves. His face, arms and legs were tanned to a lovely light golden colour; every slight movement that he made as he leaned above me there revealed a supple young strength and grace which I had never seen in any boy of his age before. He was so well formed and so beautifully proportioned that I did not then see how small he was for his age. I could not think of him in those few moments as someone who was going to grow bigger.

I heard Mrs. Sarkissian's voice from the passage and I turned to the hall again. Nuaman swung himself down beside me as softly as a cat. The two little dark-haired girls whom Mrs. Sarkissian shepherded before her were small enough, I suppose, with their prettiness, to be called doll-like. But it was their size only that suggested that; the comparison didn't dwell in my mind more than a second. The next instant I had thought of some kind of small gazelle I had seen somewhere, not in a picture, but alive. They had just the same rounded softness of body and limb combined with a surprising suppleness and grace. Like Nuaman's, their dress seemed more than is usual with English children to set off their figures rather than to cover them. Their clothes were *on* them rather than they *in* their clothes. They both wore little white sleeveless frocks of pure silk which lay smoothly to the curves of their bodies and made the sun-tan of their arms and legs glow more duskily by contrast with its gleaming whiteness. Their black hair was tied with broad ribbons and they wore white shoes and socks. They were creatures of summer and some country of the sun.

Nuaman introduced them, glancing from them to me as if he was well aware of their loveliness and proud of being able to show them off to me. They were shy, and I guessed that they did not know English or English customs so well as Nuaman for, taking my hand and murmuring their replies to me, they looked at him to see if they were doing the right thing.

"Marvan and Ianthe," Nuaman introduced them. "They both look very much alike," he added with grave simplicity, "but you can tell Marvan because she has black eyes and Ianthe because she has brown ones." He said something to them in their own language which made them lift their heads and look up at me.

"Oh, Ianthe's eyes are much too lovely to be called just brown," I said. "I should call them onyx."

"Yes?" he said, eagerly, and came across to look into them, as if he had never looked at Ianthe before. "Onyx," he repeated to himself several times, trying over the new word and treasuring it.

"Are you twins?" I asked the girls, because they both seemed so much an age and so much alike. But neither they nor Nuaman seemed to understand the word.

When we parted Nuaman touched my arm shyly, looking up into my face to see whether I minded his touching me and then, when I smiled, he clutched my hand and exclaimed with the frankest pleasure:

"You know, Miss Hazel, I *shall* like having you here!"

I went blithely in to dinner that evening with Dr Ravelin. He put me a good deal more at my ease than he had done at the interview in London. Some formality remained; or what I thought formality. Dr Ravelin wore a dinner jacket; we sat at opposite ends of a large, highly polished dark table set with fine glass and silver and embroidered table-mats; and we were waited on by Mr. Sarkissian who, in the office of footman and butler, wore a clean shirt and a dark green velvet jacket. Having seen something of the Doctor's ceremoniousness I had changed out of my suit, in which I had travelled, and put on my best dress which I had only worn about three times before; but I felt that the next night I ought to wear my evening dress and promised to make up for the demands this job would make on my wardrobe by buying myself a new evening dress out of my earnings—provided I could drive a hard enough bargain with my aunt over the coupons.

Here in his own house the little touches of formality in Dr Ravelin's speech and manners were attractive. They seemed appropriate to his style of living, to the old-fashioned house and to this air of space and leisure that was so new to me. In a clumsy, roundabout way I tried to convey this by saying how much I admired the Hall and its setting and the way it had been maintained unspoilt. I said, or tried to say, that to live in such a place, in such a way, gave a sense of continuity that was lacking in most people's lives. He listened to my stumbling remarks attentively.

"Continuity," he said. "It is a very old puzzle, isn't it? The riddle of mutability that has vexed men's minds and set them an unanswerable problem ever since the Egyptians of pre-dynastic times buried their dead crouched in the form of a question-mark! We haven't answered the question yet. It is put afresh with every death of a human being. We seek, perhaps, some partial solution of it in a generalisation, in the concept of a genus that lives though individuals die. Or some of us can, as you say, fancy that we feel the thread on which the beads are strung, by living where our fathers have lived and extending by our own short span the work of a few past generations. Or a dabbling antiquarian like myself may grope a little further and elaborate the illusion."My ancestors, Ravelins and Pocockes, have lived at Ringstones for some four hundred years. Before them men had lived in this place for perhaps six hundred years. There was a priory here which, on such imperfect evidence as exists, may be supposed to have been founded in the tenth century. Much of its fabric is knit into these walls and the bones of some of its inhabitants lie under the grass on which you will walk tomorrow. But men worked here before the monks sang. There is the shaft of a Roman lead mine in the valley, and both iron implements and bronze ornaments of Celtic pattern have been found here. Then consider the tumuli on the moor. Chieftains of the Beaker Folk? They pitched their everlasting mansions above a spot that could not then have been unknown to settlement, or at least to the seasonal camps of herdsmen and hunters. Yet before then, if I read the signs rightly, men, or beings at any rate endowed with ingenuity and imagination, resorted to this place for a purpose we can guess at though the knowledge that inspired it and the arts by which it was furthered remain dark to us. Did you observe on your way across the moor certain standing stones? They form one of those stone circles about which antiquarians will dispute for ever. A stone circle—a magic circle, if you will—but one that marks the end of our little thread of continuity. Beyond that we cannot even guess whose graves we dwell upon. Unless, indeed, we choose to fancy that we see a lesson in their circle and say we dwell upon our own."

I don't know whether my air of polite attention made Dr Ravelin think I was interested in antiquities or whether he was so absorbed in the subject himself that he could talk about nothing else. I listened all through dinner and long after dinner was over, but often I did not understand what he was talking about; there were so many references to books and names and periods that meant nothing to me, but I suppose he had forgotten that he was not talking to a fellow archaeologist. I listened without being bored because I liked his voice and liked, too, the atmosphere of crowded history with which his talk seemed to fill Ringstones; and if now and again my attention wandered from his philosophising to his own expressive face and hands and to the lovely china and silver and the fine old furniture of the dining-room, I think I did not enjoy my evening any the less for that I was receiving compensations for many years of Green Street and appreciating every minute of it.

When he at length made signs of rising I realised that he had not once mentioned the children. There was a lot now that I wanted to ask about them, but he gave me little opportunity. However, before we got up from the table, after one or two ineffectual attempts, I did succeed in mentioning Nuaman. He gave me a keen glance, then fidgeted with the things before him on the table. It had not been hard to guess that he was completely out of his element with children. He was plainly wondering what I thought about them. I reassured him gladly:

"I think they're all three delightful. I'm sure I'm going to enjoy every minute of being with them. I only hope they'll like me."

"Oh, no question of that. No question!" he exclaimed. They will keep you busy. But you mustn't let them take all your time. There are studies, no doubt of your own that you would like to pursue. Miss Corrigan, I believe, is greatly interested in biology. There are books here. I will show you the library..."

In vain I tried to keep him to the subject of the children. I wanted to know where they came from, what their language was, whether he had any particular ideas about the kind of thing we should do together. He cut all that short by rising abruptly and saying in a tone of mock consternation:

"But my dear Miss Hazell I hoped you were going to do all that! Really, I know nothing about the education of children. I have by no means completed my own education yet. Please do whatever you think suitable. I leave them entirely in your hands—or you in theirs!"

Before such abdication of responsibility I could only laugh and declare I would do my best. Nothing could have pleased me better; for the first time in my life I could do as I liked.

**4**

My breakfast was brought to me in my bedroom next morning by Mrs. Sarkissian. I protested at such unnecessary attention and said I would rather come down and have it with the children,

"They've had theirs and been out a couple of hours," she said. It was only half-past seven. I was already dressed and had been on the point of going down but I felt so guilty that I would have left my breakfast untouched in my hurry to redeem what I feared might be thought slackness. Mrs. Sarkissian, however, would not let me. I was not to worry about keeping the same hours as the children, she told me. "The young man will be up before daylight sometimes, and sometimes hell he in bed till noon. I let him do as he likes. He'll have his own way, he will."

Her face was pretty well expressionless. I could not tell whether she approved of Nuaman or not. But as she seemed disposed to be talked to I chatted to her while I gulped down my breakfast: said I hoped the children didn't make too much work for her; it seemed a big house for one person to look after.

"There's always work. But Hagop does a lot in the house. Besides, the maid'll be back in a bit."

"Your husband doesn't speak English so well as you, does he?" I asked. Except for the one word "Ringstones" uttered when he met me I hadn't heard him speak a word of English.

"He speaks it," she answered.

"But you always speak Italian together?" I said.

She gave a short laugh and said with great disdain:

"Italian? Naow! We're Armenians."

I said I supposed she must have been in England a long time.

"I been here twenty years. I came with Dr Ravelin from Aleppo before the war."

"And the children? Are they from Aleppo, too?"

She shook her head.

I went out into a dazzling summer morning. The air was fresh and cool, but the cloudless sky promised a hot day. There

was bird-song from every side and a busy squabbling of
jackdaws among the tall beeches about the house.

I had not far to look for the girls. They were sitting side by
side on the low stone wall that bounded the terrace. I had no
clear idea how I was going to set about my duties, but I thought
I ought to spend the first few days in getting to know the
children and finding out how good or bad their English was
before I could form any plan for improving it. The girls slid off
their perch and stood demurely side by side as I greeted them.
They replied 'Good morning' carefully and with a correct enough
pronunciation, but they were baffled when I went on talking to
them in an ordinary conversational way. They stood there with
their heads bent and little embarrassed smiles curving their lips,
looking as uncomfortable as I should have felt if I had suddenly
found myself being talked to, say, by a Frenchwoman in French.
The best beginning, I thought, was to get them all together, so
I asked where Nuaman was. That, or the name (though I know
I didn't pronounce it right) they understood and Ianthe, the
brown-eyed one, pointed down the park.

They would have fallen in behind me, but, talking all the
time in the hope of overcoming their shyness, I made them walk
one on each side of me, and in that way, with an occasional
gesture from one of them to show the way, we crossed towards
the beck.

The turf we walked on was close and soft and springy,
cropped short by the sheep more efficiently than if it had been
tended by a professional groundsman. For a wide space before
the house it was perfectly level. There was all the room one
could desire for games, and as we walked along I was already
planning what we could play with four people. The beck flows
more towards the east side of the park, that is, the side away
from where the road from Blagill comes down, and its course is
marked by a line of various trees: alders, willows, mountain-ash,
poplars, limes and birches. Beyond it, where the ground is not
too steep and rocky to give them root-hold, there are plantations
of pine and larch which climb the hillside until they thin out into
scattered copses or huddled groups of trees all leaning together
and straining away from the whip of the wind. At the bottom of
the park, beyond a little oak-wood, the beck plunges between
two towering crags and then rushes down a deep wooded glen

on its way to join the river Nither.

I saw all this under the golden light of one of those mornings that compensate in one deep breath of their intoxicating air for endless winters of rain and drizzle and heavy skies and grimy fog. I felt that my eyes could never see enough of those innumerable shades of green, nor my ears have their fill of birdsong and the loud, long music of the water. I could feel the strengthening sun begin to pour on my neck and arms, and I smelt the warm sweetness of the deep old turf and all its tiny flowers. I had the absurd fancy that such a morning had never been known before in England; that these children, sun-browned themselves, clad as though to offer their bodies to the sun, had brought a richer and more splendid warmth with them from their Eastern home to this little hollow of the North.

When we reached the bank of the stream I could still not see Nuaman. Without hesitation the two girls jumped down and crossed the foaming water on the boulders. I followed and we turned down the farther bank. The turf grew coarser here and the ground was softer and damper. We picked our way among tufts of rushes and clumps of bog-myrtle and round cushions of moss stitched all over with tiny stars of white flowers. Here grew tall yellow flags and such a profusion of spotted orchises as I have never seen elsewhere. Marvan and Ianthe, wearing sandals, splashed unconcernedly through the wet places, but I, being careful of my shoes and socks, stepped more warily, picking out the clumps of rushes and occasional dark grey stones for my footing. Looking down in this way I did not see Nuaman until we were almost upon him.

He was sitting cross-legged on a large flat-topped boulder that overhung the beck. He looked up at our approach, which I am certain he had heard or seen long before I saw him, and cried, "Good morning, Miss Hazel!" cheerfully; then he bent his head again over some, little contraption that he was busy making out of reeds and twigs. I sprang up on to the rock beside him and glanced down into the stream hurrying away among its stones, then at the boy's short dark curls and bent back.

There was nothing ill-mannered in Nuaman's preoccupation with his handiwork. I felt, rather, that after our recognition of friendship the night before he accepted me as an understanding companion with whom ceremony was out of place. I watched him while he worked. He had left off his shirt, and the sunlight, broken by the leaves of an alder that grew beside the rock, patterned the clear gold of his naked skin. He was tanned very evenly, as if he had spent most of his time running about undressed in the sun. He wore nothing on his feet, which were well-shaped and strong. He had been used to going barefoot, I guessed, since his infancy.

He worked very deftly with fingers that looked both strong and sensitive. It was a little cage he was making and it was put together with extraordinary ingenuity and skill.

"What are you going to put in your cage?" I asked.

He twisted his head round and looked up at me with a quick smile.

"I don't know yet I must see what I can catch. Perhaps a squirrel."

"It's not big enough," I said. "But are there squirrels in your country, too?"

"Oh yes," he answered, putting his work aside. "Yes, there are squirrels in my country."

"What is your country, Nuaman?"

"No," he said. "Not Nu-a-man. You must say it like this." He laughed and pronounced his name several times, urging me to repeat it and clapping his hands when I got somewhere near the right pronunciation. He made a queer little stop in his throat just after the V, which I couldn't imitate well enough to please him, but I succeeded in drawing out the last syllable until he approved. Then he asked me what my other name was.

"Daphne," he repeated. "That's an old name, isn't it? Nearly as old as mine. Look! Let's go and look for a squirrel!"

"Aren't you going to tell me about your country?"

"Oh, another time. Do come and look at the squirrel's house that we've found."

He jumped up and called something softly to the girls who were loitering by the foot of the tree near us; then, like a squirrel himself, he slipped from the rock and in two bounds was across the stream.

I had come out with the intention of collecting the children and taking charge of them but, instead, I found myself following Nuaman on a dancing, darting tour of the park. He went over the ground like a hare in March or an untrained spaniel pup, ranging back and forth to examine here a tree, there a tuffet of moss or a flower. He was as talkative as the girls were silent The words came tumbling from him, sometimes in perfectly easy, colloquial English, at other times queerly misused or wrongly combined so that I was puzzled to grasp his meaning. I could see his need for someone to practise his English with, but, as I tried to keep up with his will-o'-the-wisp career across the park, I also agreed rather grimly with Dr Ravelin that no one but a budding gym-teacher would do.

He led us in the end to the edge of the oak-wood at the lower end of the park, and there he leaned, laughing, against the trunk of a tall, straight oak.

"There now, do you see the squirrel-house?" he asked.

High up among the leaves I could make out something that might have been a large nest of twigs and grass. Whether it was a squirrel's or some large bird's I could not say. I had no idea whether there were squirrels in that part or not.

"Shall I go and see if the children are still there?" Nuaman asked.

"The children? Oh, I see. The young ones, you mean. Why, I don't know. Would there be young ones at this time of the year? But you can't climb that, can you?"

The bole of the oak was straight and too thick for him to swarm up, while the first branch grew out a good twelve or fourteen feet from the ground. I myself could not have reached it with a standing jump. Nuaman trotted back some yards from the tree, paused an instant and before I had grasped what he was going to do he dashed at the trunk, leaped and touched it with his toes six feet from the ground and with the momentary purchase he gained there sprang up and caught the horizontal bough. In a minute he was among the higher branches and hidden by the leaves. I heard him call out, laughing, "The children, I mean the young ones, are not in the house!"

Now, I thought, this is the real test of my qualifications. Sure enough, in a moment Nuaman was calling out to me, "Oh, do come up, Daphne!" I could have climbed the tree, but I could not have run up it the way he had done. At least, not without a few trial shots. The two girls, as I saw out of the corner of my eye, were looking at me expectantly. I called out that I couldn't come up in the frock and shoes I had on then, but I would climb as many trees as he liked when I was properly dressed for it. He seemed to be perfectly satisfied and clambered swiftly down, swinging himself lightly off the lowest branch. There was not the slightest hint of showing-off in his manner: not even the faint, polite contempt an English boy of his age would have for a girl who would wear such stupid clothes that she couldn't do things.

I got them back into the house and began to talk about what we should do. My chief interest just then was in finding out something about them. But always Nuaman darted away from the subject of his country, his parents and his language. Even the length of his stay at Ringstones he would not state exactly.

"Oh, we've been here a long time. Years," he said lightly.

"All summer?" I persisted, interpreting the exaggeration.

"Yes, all the summer."

I say *he* would not tell me. Even so early I realised that it was he and not the girls who was to be my chief concern. They were for the most part quite silent; all I could get out of them for a long time was a 'yes' or 'no' given, I generally felt, without any understanding of the question. I did, however, satisfy myself to some extent about their relations to Nuaman.

"You're not brother and sisters," I had asked direct.

"Oh no, not that."

"Cousins, then?"

"Cousins? I don't understand. What are cousins?"

I explained. "Yes, yes!" he said, when I had disentangled myself from degrees of kinship more complicated than I had realised before trying to define them. "Yes, something of the sort." And as if repeating the lesson to Marvan and Ianthe he rattled away to them for a minute or two in their own language quoting the word 'cousin' and impressing it upon them, as it seemed.

We spent all that day together, indoors and out, ranging into every part of the park, peeping into every room of the old house except only Dr Ravelin's own. I was amazed at Nuaman's acute observation and knowledge of English birds and animals and flowers. Often, it is true, he did not know the English names, and I had to confess my own ignorance so often that I grew ashamed of myself, but he seemed to know them all in his own language and to distinguish every one without hesitation.

Marvan and Ianthe followed us in cur comings and goings, always reserved and shy and a little behind. He gave them little orders—or what seemed to be orders— in their language, always softly and gaily, and they obeyed promptly, fetching and carrying for him as an English girl might fetch and carry for an adored brother years younger than herself. I had learned, however, that Nuaman and the girls were the same age.

On the whole I remember feeling well content when my first day's work ended at the children's supper time. I went up to my room and surveyed my day. It had been a strenuous one, and there was one more strenuous thing yet to do. I had to meet Nuaman's challenge. Luckily I had sent on all my clothes to Ringstones. I put on my gym shorts and a jersey and a pair of gym shoes and slipped out into the park while the children were still at supper and Dr Ravelin was still in his study.

I found the oak tree again without difficulty. I paced back about as far as Nuaman had done and studied the thing. I had never attempted anything quite like it before, and I could see that it needed good judgment if I was not to bungle it or hurt myself. Then, as I looked at the trunk of the tree, I saw there was something that made it a little easier: a slight, rounded projection at about the six foot mark. That, I decided, after examining it at close quarters, was where Nuaman had got his foothold. I drew back again and went at it. I did better than I expected; I got my foot on the projecting knob but missed my grip on the branch above me. Still, I sprang backwards and landed on my feet without damage. I timed it better the next time and got a good grip on the branch with both hands. From there it was just like an exercise on the beam in the gym, though I wished for my arms' and legs' sake that the branch had been as smooth as the beam. It was easy enough to climb up to the nest at the top of the tree, but, just to make sure that I could do it quickly the next day, I went up and down again. I stood on the lowest branch again, holding lightly on with one hand and surveying my knees and elbows before jumping down. Then I started so that I all but lost my balance when a soft voice said:

"They haven't come back? No, I don't expect they will. I saw them in the wood."

There he was, dressed now in his green shorts and cream shirt, squatting on the grass below and looking up at me like a

# 34 Ringstones

good-natured little goblin.

I lowered myself and sat on the branch and said, "Well?"

"I've just finished my supper," he said. "Shall we go climbing now?"

"Aha!" I said. "Now I'm dressed for it and you're not. We'll climb tomorrow. Just now I'm going to go and wash off this moss and black and make myself respectable for dinner."

"Yes, your dress is very good," he remarked gravely. "I like it. You must wear it always."

"It looks as if I shall need to," I said. "But I think I shall prefer a pair of slacks if mere is much tree-climbing on the programme. I hadn't realised my skin came off so easily."

"You know," he said, when I had swung myself down and we were walking back to the house. "I like girls who can make facts."

"Make facts?" I repeated, quite baffled.

"Why yes. To jump up to that branch is quite a fact."

"Oh, I see. You mean a feat. We say, make feats. No we don't. We say, to do feats."

He murmured the words over to himself for a time: fact, feat, fact, feat. Then asked:

"Is making a squirrel cage a fact or a feat?"

"Lord!" I said. "Well, I suppose it's a fact that you made it and it would be a feat if I made it."

He laughed, and in spite of his previous mistake I'm sure he saw what I meant.

"Well, but Marvan and Ianthe," I asked him. "Can they do feats, as you call it?"

"Oh yes, they can," he replied. "Katia's the one who's not really very good at that kind of feat. But she can run. I hope you will run with me tomorrow."

"Who on earth is Katia?" I demanded.

He gave me a wondering look. "Why, Katia who puts the things on the table and makes the beds and helps Mrs. Sarkissian."

"The maid? But she's away, isn't she?"

"Yes, she's away at present," he replied without much interest. "But look, will you run a race with me tomorrow? With me and Ianthe, if you like?"

He wheedled and insisted so that I had to promise. I reckon

myself as good as anybody in the Junior year at Towerton over four-forty yards, but from what I had already seen of Nuaman I foresaw, without any doubt at all, that I should be only a fair second to him.

## 5

A fair second. While I hesitated what course to adopt with the children my role was given me by Nuaman. I may have wondered in what capacity exactly I had come to Ringstones and what I ought to be doing to earn my thirty pounds, but he had no doubts at all: I was to be his playmate. It suited me. I don't think I've ever enjoyed any organised games one half so much as the boundless fun of tearing about that Park with Nuaman. I'd never had such a chance to run wild before and I didn't give a hoot that I was behaving more like fifteen than nineteen.

Only in the evenings, dining with Dr Ravelin, and having disguised myself as a young lady, did I have occasional twinges of conscience. I never saw the Doctor in the daytime. He said he kept to his study all day; yet I felt he must now and then catch sight of me and the children in our chasing about the place. He had never commented on the way I behaved and I did not suppose that he expected from a girl of these days the deportment of one of Jane Austen's young ladies, but I certainly had a feeling that the spectacle of me prancing about the park in my skimpy gym trunks or my short Towerton tunic, which I wore most of the time, might jar on him. Might he not, glimpsing me racing bare-legged over the grass, have a wistful vision of long satin skirts sweeping that same grass and the ample folds of a furbelowed frock billowing with decorous grace upon it as ladies picnicked there long ago?

I need not have worried. I discovered that he had quite other visions of the forms that had paced his park before us.

He proposed one evening that we should take a stroll. We went from the table, he in his formal black suit and starched shirt and I in my evening frock, and in the rich light of the sun that was just touching the edge of Ringstones Moor we walked slowly across the grass barred with the shadows of the trees.

The stillness and peace of the evening were complete. The three kinds of sounds I recall seemed only to emphasise by their distinctness the purity of the silence that they cut: the clear song of thrushes in the ash-tree tops; the ceaseless monologue of the running water, and the far-carrying bawling—there is no other word for it—of a well-grown lamb from the hill.

"Do you see," said Dr Ravelin, when we had reached a point about the middle of the level ground of the park. "Do you see how the curve of the beck here seems to enclose a natural amphitheatre? Think of it as it must have appeared before the trees were planted. A level, almost circular tract of sward, always green. See how the side of the hill there curves in a great bank round the Western half of the circle. You would say a natural auditorium from which many thousands of spectators could look down into this arena. In Homer's Greece such a spot would have seen the funeral games of Kings. Heroes and Cods themselves might have sat here to watch the athletes race and hurl the discus. What splendid footing for the wrestlers this ancient turf would give!"

He smiled, and moved a few paces away across the turf.

"These fancies, you know, are not unrelated to the facts, though they may outrun them. Not far away there to the South is a Roman camp. Here in the valley is a Roman mine which shows evidence of having been worked for many years. There was undoubtedly a considerable population in the neighbourhood in Roman times: labourers, soldiers, engineers, officers, functionaries. Would the possibilities of such a spot as this escape the eye of a Roman officer? Was the Roman army on duty at the limits of the Empire less likely to organise its familiar sports than the British Army in Egypt or in China?

"Look," he said. He had paused at a spot I had noticed often before, where a big flat stone buried in the ground made the only break in the level lawn. "Look round from this stone. It is the centre of this level area of the Park and the circumference of the circle is almost exactly a Roman mile. You may run a Roman mile round the Park on even, firm turf."

I confessed that I had done.

"I have galloped it often when I was a boy," he said. "Old John Pococke, who planted the Park, left that strip all round the circumference clear of trees as if he intended it for a ride or race-track. Or," he added, after a pause, cocking his head and looking at me slyly, "or as if he knew it was one.

"Oh no," he went on, hastily. "I don't say there is any evidence. I'm only too conscious that I look at this place with the eye of faith, which sees what may not be there. If I think I see the turf very slightly depressed in that circuit and if I think I can discern the faint lines of what may be been a retaining bank, I am quite ready to admit that I am deceiving myself and that the chariots have whirled round this arena only in my fancy."

I remember the sun had now dipped behind Ringstones Moor and we saw the rough hillside where Dr Ravelin pictured the ancient spectators of the games under the shadow of approaching twilight which shed on it a cool gravity of grey-green and blue-grey tones. Still there was a pale golden refulgence above the hill that sent distinct rays, like the spokes of a wheel, branching up into the deepening blue of the sky above our heads; and the tips of the topmost twisted pines on the other hill, behind us, glowed softly still.

Dr Ravelin stared up into the Western sky, at those far-stretching rays, and it was some time before he spoke again.

"But the Romans seem little remoter than our own great-grandfathers when we think by comparison of the eyes that must have watched, with the intentness of a holy purpose, these same rays of sunset or sunrise from this spot where we are standing. This place was holy an unthinkable age before the Romans came. Where we see these rays unterminating, diffusing rather and losing themselves in space and light, those eyes saw each ray tipped with the figure of unending life. An arm of the sun extended to them the holy Ankh. That is not fancy. Or if it is fancy it is one whose antiquity is recorded in stony fact. Perhaps you can't distinguish it now in this light, but look tomorrow morning, you will see on the hillside there a long, sloping line roughly parallel with our drive that comes down from the track across Ringstones Moor. It is the trace of a causeway which led in very ancient times up from this level arena to the moor top; up to the stone circle. There, in that complex of standing stones, are set the altar-stone and sun-stone aligned to look into the eye of the sun when he rises from behind this Eastern moor."

He talked about megalithic monuments, heliacal rites and

a great deal of other learned matters while we sauntered back to the house. He was talking more to himself than to me.

"Guesses, guesses!" he exclaimed suddenly when, having reached the terrace, we turned to look back over the park. "But someone *knew*. The explanation was here. The road from the stone circle leads back into the park. Something here has laughed at all those priests and laughs still at all our learned arguments."

He left me with a quick smile and a change of tone: "My fancies may seem strange to you, Miss Hazel, but you might be no stranger among them if they were embodied."

**6**

In and out among Dr Ravelin's talk of ancient times and foreign lands I threaded the name of Nuaman, but I was never able to pin the Doctor down to a clear statement of who and what he was. Really, I suppose, I did not persist The mere name of his country would probably not have conveyed much to me. It certainly could not have added to my delight in that mingling of gaiety and gravity, wisdom and mischief and those astonishing gifts of physical beauty and agility for which I had begun to love Nuaman. His qualities seemed to have as little to do with the map as they had with the calendar. Just as he could behave like a child one minute and like a mature man the next, so by turns I could fancy him as native English as myself or a Prince from some fairytale country beyond the seas.

Dr Ravelin smiled at this. "Ah, these labels of age and place! They only stick when we grow old. And yet, you know, children are really the ancients among us. It is we, the older people, who bear the stamp of temporariness, the impress of a brief, particular period: we, with our clothes of a particular fashion, our manners dictated by the conventions of our generation, our heads packed full of the prejudices, called information, peculiar to the particular time at which we were educated. We are like a bit of complicated modern machinery, a motor-car or a wireless set. We are the latest thing this year; next year sees one little part modified and our model becomes obsolete. Children are nearer to the essence of life. They are unspecialised humanity. Which of us, do you think, Nuaman or I, would feel sooner at home if we were tomorrow by some freak of time to walk into a gathering of the ancient inhabitants of this valley? It is obvious enough. The complex is ephemeral and at the mercy of the least disturbance. The simple is, broadly speaking, immutable and infused with the quality of duration. What you discern in Nuaman are the qualities of youth, and, at the heart, those qualities move us with the same feeling as does the spectacle of great antiquity. No, as would immortality itself if we could see it embodied. Youth is an attribute of the Gods, and a gleam of godhead shines in every youthful face. You are not so old, Miss Hazel, but that you may confirm that in your own glass."

I looked in my glass, and saw two blue eyes, moderately bright, and a pair of cheeks a good deal browner than they had ever been before; I looked in the long mirror in the bathroom and saw a figure that caused me no qualms about its fitness. But that did not explain Nuaman. Nor could, or would, Nuaman explain himself.

He was too restless for me ever to keep him in conversation for more than a minute or two at a time, and even then his talk, like his actions, was darting, dancing, bewildering. He wanted speed and spring and wild exertion in everything he did. Neither his cousins nor I could ever go fast enough or keep up a game long enough for him. Sometimes, when I refused to move any more and he reluctantly granted his cousins a respite, he would make Sarkissian bring out the fierce little pony and would ride it bare-backed at a furious gallop round the circular grass drive of the park. He did not even use a halter and the pony's mane was clipped too short for him to grip, but though it bucked and reared and shied nothing could unseat Nuaman once he had gripped with his bare legs. Once, when we were on the hillside, a big ram jumped up, startled, out of a hollow. Nuaman sprang after it, caught it and mounted it. The ram, being half wild, went mad and bolted down the steep slope, clearly bent on suicide. I shrieked helplessly after Nuaman; then, an instant before they reached the rocks where they would both have broken their necks, he rolled off, and the ram, with a swerving bound, missed the precipice and fled along the hill above. It was impossible to scold or control Nuaman. I did not even try. Telling him to be careful would have been as pointless as telling a monkey not to fall out of a tree. In his most daring feats he knew exactly what he was doing. It was obvious, too, that he knew his cousins' abilities as accurately as he knew his own. He exacted from them the very last ounce of energy in every game we played, but never forced them or dared them to do anything that was beyond them.

I teased him about his command over them. I called him their Lord and Master, the King of Ringstones, the Slave-Driver. He laughed and they went on slavishly obeying him, and so, for that matter, did I.

We had thrown ourselves down one day in the shade of a chestnut tree. I asked him questions about his country and his people—more for the sake of keeping him still for a few minutes than out of real curiosity. But he would not be serious.

"This is my country! Ringstones is my country!" he said, and lay on his back and laughed. "Well, then," I said. "What's your other name?" Then he did become for a moment grave, or pretended to be grave. "We never tell our real names," he said very solemnly. "People say a man must never say his real name out loud because if he did *they* might hear and they would have power over him." His eyes were twinkling again as he said that.

"They? Who do you mean by 'they'?"

"Oh, you know…" He shrugged his shoulders. Then laughed so much he set Marvan and Ianthe giggling and squirming about on the grass half hysterical at the mysterious joke.

"But what about Nuaman?" I persisted. "That's your real name, isn't it?"

The two girls rolled about and gurgled and choked and snorted with laughter until Nuaman, laughing so much himself that he could hardly speak, threw green horse-chestnuts at them and finally half quietened them with a slap before they wriggled out of reach. "Aren't they a badly-behaved pair?" he said, screwing up his face to stop his own laughter.

I looked at the pair, kneeling on the grass, stuffing their fists into their mouths and still heaving with their fit of the giggles.

"Well, you started them off," I said, wondering what on earth it was all about.

"I started them off!" he cried. "Right! I'll stop them!" Quick as eels they eluded his spring and dodged in different directions behind the trees. He caught Marvan by the frock in a twinkling. I rushed to defend her—or her frock, and so that attempt at a conversation too ended in a wild game of catch-as-catch-can.

Nuaman rarely spent more than half his day with me; though as his day sometimes began at dawn and ended in the small hours, what I thought was a half was probably nearer a fifth. He would sometimes yawn lazily like a cat when I found him curled up somewhere in the morning sunlight and confess that he had been out all night. A lot of the time he was not with me he spent with Sarkissian in the old stables. He always refused to tell me what he did there, but I gathered Sarkissian had a workshop there and I supposed that Nuaman, with his own skill in making things, liked to hang about and watch and help. Sarkissian was as much his slave as anybody. I asked Dr Ravelin one evening.

"The old stables?" he repeated. "Well, you may call them old. They cover, in fact, the site of the priory. Old Squire John pulled the ruins down and used the stone to build this house, but a good deal of the original foundation remains there. I have traced the cloister. But what interests me more is that there are distinct indications that the priory itself was built on the foundations of a much earlier edifice. Without doing far more work than I am able to undertake it is impossible to establish the matter beyond doubt, but I have the strongest suspicions that some work which may be Roman, but I think much older, lies under the masonry there. One day I must take you and show you what I base my beliefs on. It's highly interesting."

I felt no doubt it was, but I hardly thought that that was what interested Nuaman. Dr Ravelin forgot to take me and Nuaman clearly did not want me to go, so I never went inside the great old gates of the stable-yard.

Then, unexpectedly, I saw one of the products of the work-shop. The children had gobbled their lunch and run out to the park. I sat drinking a cup of tea and gossiping with Mrs. Sarkissian for half an hour or so, and then I strolled out after them. I had not far to seek them. From behind a long clump of rhododendrons a short distance from the house I heard the girls squealing excitedly and Nuaman shouting. But mingled with their voices was the most extraordinary mooing, moaning sound, like a calf with its voice breaking. I ran round the end of the clump and stopped dead.

Bent double and frisking about the open space, emitting all the time those unearthly whoops, was a fair-haired girl of about my own age. Her only garment seemed to be a brown boiler-suit, and that several sizes too small for her. The straps were strained across her bare back, and from the stern view, which was my first, it looked as if a seam might split disastrously at any moment. To that stern was pinned a length of old rope with the end frayed out to represent a tail, and as the girl swung round her head appeared decorated with a pair of fearsome, spreading cow's horns. She was playing the part of a pantomime cow gone mad and putting terrific zest into the performance; and there, dancing round her was Nuaman in his white bathing slips and the two girls in their little brightly patterned trunks and halters. In another second I made mental apologies to the "cow". The game was a bullfight, and an extraordinary one at that. The "bull" charged straight at Nuaman with lowered horns and every appearance of intending to go straight through him. But he, instead of skipping out of the way like a matador, launched himself with outstretched arms in a remarkable, dog-like leap clean over the oncoming "bull's" head. Then, as he skimmed over, my heart missed a beat, for the "bull" viciously swung up its horns, missing his unprotected stomach by a matter of inches. I shouted out, but the game was going too fast: Nuaman landed and sprang away; the "bull" turned and charged again, and this time it was Marvan who sailed over the up-slashing horns.

"Nuaman!" I yelled.

The game stopped and the children came rushing up to me while the older girl slowly straightened up and turned to stare at me with a pair of light blue eyes in a broad, placid face that was very cow-like indeed.

"This is Katia," cried Nuaman, pulling me forward and taking both of us by the hand. I had forgotten all about Katia. No one had breathed a word about her having come back Nuaman pulled us down to sit on a little mound, one on each side of him. Katia undid the horned apparatus from her head. Her hair was short and bleached-looking, lighter than her sun-browned skin. She was a robust, strong-looking girl.

"Katia?" I said to her across Nuaman who leaned back on his elbows, grinning away. "And where have you sprung from?"

"Please?" she asked blankly in the most un-English of accents.

"I mean where do you come from?" I said, more slowly.

She put her hands on her round thighs and leaned forward gazing at me earnestly and sadly.

"I am day pay," she said.

"Day pay?" I said. "Do you mean you come by the day?"

She seemed to consider how to explain it.

"You say, dippee," she announced.

"Dippy!" I exclaimed, and I believe I began to edge away. "What on earth...?"

She turned her head and contemplated the park for a bit, and then, with a sigh and a shrug, as if admitting the worst, "I am a displeased parson," she said.

They say you have to humour them, I thought, and it was on the tip of my tongue to reply that I was the Pope of Rome and not amused, when light dawned. In some ten minutes of questioning at the wildest cross-purposes I discovered—or thought I did—that she was a Pole who had suffered some complicated displacements during and since the war. We might have got further but I heard Mrs. Sarkissian's voice calling from beyond the shrubs. Katia, exclaiming "My God!" jumped up and fled with the chewed-looking tail still swinging behind her.

Nuaman looked at me and then flung himself on his back and hooted with laughter. I picked up the horned head-gear. It was well-contrived, with the horns fixed on two thin, curved metal bands and a strap to go under the chin and another round the back of the head. The tips of the horns were quite sharp. I looked down at the soft skin of Nuaman's naked tummy and shuddered. I should have a word in private with Katia about this game, I decided.

"Where on earth did you pick up such a dangerous game as this?" I asked.

He took the horns from me. "Oh, it's an old game, that. It's only dangerous with a real bull. But doesn't Katia make a wonderful she-bull?" The memory of her antics convulsed him.

I looked round for his cousins. They had disappeared.

"I say!" he exclaimed, suddenly sitting up. "It's good, isn't it? Now you and Katia are both here."

"Oh, is it? Why?"

"Well, I like you both."

I asked him where Marvan and Ianthe were.

"They've gone up to the pool to bathe. Then they're going to wrestle. We shall watch them wrestling if you care. But perhaps you don't care for wrestling?*

He seemed so disappointed when I told him that I didn't that to cheer him up I promised to show him some day what I knew about ju-jitsu. That was a mistake, because he was all for having me demonstrate there and then. I could only get out of that by pointing out that we weren't evenly enough matched. He thought for a moment and then started up eagerly as an idea struck him.

"I say! You match Katia!" he exclaimed.

"Oh, so that's why it's good that Katia and I are both here? And what would Miss Katia say, I wonder, if I challenged her to a wrestling match for your amusement? And we don't say 'you match someone', we say 'you are a match for someone'."

"Yes? But there's another match, isn't there? I mean you and Katia are both the same height, nearly the same weight and you have fair hair and blue eyes and so has she, and when you have been here a bit longer your skin will be the same colour as hers. Isn't that right?"

"Well," I said, "I suppose the *fact* is right. And you could say that if we were a pair of horses. But you can't say one person matches another—even displeased persons. Anyway, match or no match, my friend, you're not going to match me against Katia at wrestling, so there!"

He grinned. "At running, then?"

"Nuaman," I said. "I do believe your spiritual home *is* the Arena."

That, too, was ill-considered, because he promptly wanted to know what the Arena was. "I thought you wanted to go and watch your cousins wrestle," I said. "Oh, never mind them," he cried. "Sit down and tell me!" So down I had to sit again and rack my brains to recollect all I had ever read about Roman games and gladiators, while he sat, clasping his knees in his arms and resting his cheek on them, listening intently.

## 7

He had his way. Katia and I did race before she had been
back at Ringstones long. She seemed to be even more at his
beck and call than his two cousins. Heaven knows how she and
he understood each other. They talked in what they no doubt
thought was English, but it might as well have been Russian for
the little I understood of it. When I tried to talk to her I always
had the feeling that both of us were capering on the giddy verge
of lunacy. And yet we got on. She was as amateurish a maid as
I was a governess, and she dealt with the housework, or as
much of it as Mrs. Sarkissian would trust her with, in the same
unpredictable fashion as she dealt with the English language.
By afternoon she had always managed to get herself dismissed
from the house, and once outside the door she would kick off
her shoes and flee from domestic slavery to fling herself into a
slavery far more abject at Nuaman's feet. She called him No
Man; and in his absence, usually Sir No Man.

We raced round the park. Katia was strong, and I fancy she
must have run a pretty wild career in whatever Polish forest she
had been allowed to grow up in. She ran barefoot and I lent her
my second pair of shorts which, for all Nuaman's saying we
"matched", she distended rather more than I hope I do. First we
raced with Nuaman and he beat us both. Then he would have
Katia and me race each other. I was for refusing, but Katia
pulled me up from the grass where I had stretched myself to get
my wind. At that moment I almost wrestled with her without the
formality of a challenge. There was no escape, one way or the
other Nuaman would have his way! So we ran, and Nuaman
loped along behind us as if driving us on, and I won by about a
yard.

Now that there were four of us Nuaman's ingenuity in
finding things to keep us on the go surpassed all previous
flights. My contribution was everything I had learned at
Towerton, but still it wasn't enough. I was the only one who did
not let him have things entirely his own way. For instance, I
stopped the bull-fighting game; but not by telling Katia she was

not to play. I tried that and found it was hopeless. She *had* to if Nuaman said so, she kept insisting. "Hang what Nuaman says," I cried in exasperation. "You're *not* to!"

"But he *must* me!" she howled in a desperate effort to convince me. So I asked Nuaman bluntly to stop it. He agreed at once, as he always did when he saw that I had made up my mind firmly about something. Perhaps my mind didn't always stay made up; but I did stick to that. I would not allow the bull-fighting, and I would not wrestle.

I still tried to keep together some shreds of a pretence of teaching the children English, and fortunately Nuaman's frequent absences gave me a chance to make some progress with the girls. Their English, as I had suspected, was not at all bad. It was simply that when they were with Nuaman, or even with each other, they were afraid of making mistakes and being laughed at. If I got one of them by herself she would talk more.

One morning Nuaman was nowhere to be found. He had been busy for a few days down in the old stables and I was wondering what new device he was going to bring forth. I wandered round the park looking for the girls and found Marvan, sitting alone beside the beck, making rosettes out of the pith of rushes.

"Where's Ianthe?" I asked. She said she thought she must have gone with "him" (meaning Nuaman). I sat down beside her and began to talk. She listened with her dark head bent, occasionally shooting a sidelong smiling glance at me. Soon I was asking her about her home and her people.

"His people?" she asked, and hesitated. "Oh, he has lots of people," she said, and then, casually, "You'll see."

"Why?" I said, very surprised. "Are they coming here?"

She shrugged her shoulders. "Of course. They live here really, but they are away just now. I wish they would come soon."

"Do you mean they are coming to live *here*, with Dr Ravelin?"

She nodded, busy with her little rosette. "I shall be glad when they come back," she went on. "It is happier when there are many people and it is not so hard. I do not have to think what to say and do."

"You mean you won't have to talk English when you don't

want to! But tell me, who's coming? Your parents?"

"Oh, all of them, I expect," she said. I had a vision of a numerous family of foreign fathers and mothers, uncles, aunts and cousins, descending on Dr Ravelin and I was puzzled. The house was big enough, but it hardly seemed the sort of thing he would want. However, before I could get anything more explicit out of Marvan, Nuaman himself came through the trees and across to us.

"Hallo!" I said. "Marvan tells me you're expecting your people to come soon. I hadn't heard about that."

He frowned slightly as if he hadn't quite grasped what I meant. Then he said something in their own language to Marvan. She looked up with a startled, almost guilty air, and was obviously about to reply when he spoke again, more sharply, and she bent her head very close over her handwork, hiding her face.

Nuaman stretched himself on the grass at my feet; he plucked a blade and chewed it, looking at me meanwhile in a comical way. "They'll say anything, those two," he remarked. "They tell awful fibs. Don't you?"

Marvan nodded her head penitently without looking up.

"Oh well," I said, "perhaps she only wishes they would come. After all, it's perhaps a long time since you've seen your people."

He yawned widely. "I say," he said. "Do you know I've only just had my breakfast?"

It was nearly lunch time. I got up and we all walked back to the house together.

Katia loved swimming. She waylaid me in the hall as we went in and while the children ran upstairs she proposed a trip to the pool in the afternoon. I said we would all go.

Nuaman didn't want any lunch. The girls were late coming down for theirs, but they never ate very much at midday. That day, I remember, they were a shorter time than ever over their lunch. Marvan fidgeted and sulked and Ianthe giggled and teased her, and as soon as I mentioned swimming the pair of them flew off to be at the pool before us.

Later, while I was waiting until Katia was ready, I went in search of Nuaman. I ran him to earth in his room. He was curled up on his bed, fast asleep. I suppose he had been roaming

about most of the night. He did not stir, but he opened his eyes
and was wide awake before I reached his bedside.

"Come on!" I said. "We're all going swimming."

He stretched his arms and legs out stiffly, just like an
animal, and smiled and shook his head, quite obviously
enjoying his nap much too much to stir. I couldn't budge him.

"Oh, well," I said, "I dare say we can do without you. We
shall have more peace. I can teach Marvan and Ianthe the
crawl."

He suddenly sat bolt upright and smacked his forehead
with his palm—a trick he copied, with exaggeration, from Katia.
"I'd forgotten that!" he exclaimed.

"Forgotten what?"

He chuckled softly and thought for a moment, then
snuggled down again.

"It doesn't matter," he said. "Remember, they tell awful
fibs." He grinned and shut his eyes tight and pretended to be so
fast asleep that I left him.

Katia was waiting for me on the terrace. She conveyed, with
several wild linguistic lunges, that we should not be late back
for tea. Nuaman wanted her for something.

"Why," I demanded, "must you always obey Nuaman so
abjectly?"

When I had finally got this into a form of words that she
more or less understood she made her blue eyes round and
serious.

"Because if not he *weep*," she declared.

I derided the idea. "Weep? Nuaman weep? What nonsense!"

She protested it was true, but I just laughed. She waved her
arms about and tried to convince me by opening her eyes so
wide and nodding her head so hard that I half expected to see
her shake her blue orbs out on to the grass.

"He do! He do!" she cried, stuttering in her effort, to carry
conviction. "He make Sarkissian weep!"

The thought of the surly, blue-chinned Armenian shedding
tears for Nuaman's waywardness was too funny for words, but
Heaven knows what fantastic notions existed in the
impenetrable jungle of Katia's mind.

The pool in which we swam, or rather splashed, was in the
narrow glen beyond the house where the, beck came tumbling

down among great rocks before reaching the level of the park. At one point the water flowed over a great, flat, greenish rock and then spouted sheer down fifteen or twenty feet to foam into a natural basin beneath. From there it poured into a deeply scooped hollow, one side of which was a sheer brown crag and the other a Up of lovely soft green turf. The side of the glen behind this bank of turf was hollowed out and the hollow screened by a thicket of birches, making a little arbour which I used for a dressing-room. The high, steep sides of the glen sheltered the place completely from the wind, unless it blew due North, and on a summer afternoon such as we were then having, the sun blazed down, heating turf and rock until one could lie and bask there as people do on a Mediterranean beach. It was a private place: the only way into it was by a faint path up the glen, partly along the steep sides, where one found a goat's footing on the heather roots, and partly over the very boulders among which the beck tumbled and foamed.

As we scrambled up and came out on to the strip of turf I heard from the squealing and laughing that was going on that Marvan and Ianthe were already in the pool. Then I saw their naked glistening bodies twisting and turning and shining brown in the clear amber water as quick as otters or seals. Katia flung down her towel and stripped off her clothes in a trice. When she saw me deliberately unrolling my costume from my towel, she cried: "Bad pants! Niet! No man shall come here but No Man!"

Having put on my costume, I loitered on the grass before diving. It was on this strip of turf, I supposed, that Nuaman used to come and watch his cousins wrestle after their bathe. Supple and shining as they climbed from the pool they might have been little models of those ancient athletes Dr Ravelin had fancied contending on such springy turf; or models, at any rate, of Diana's maidens or Penthesilea's. And, indeed, their clothes—the only sign of the century—being off, there was nothing there in that place of rocks and water, turf and trees, all the same as when the world began, to prove that the fancy was only a fancy.

Katia's bleached locks had appeared above the surface. I curled my toes round the soft edge and smiled at the two girls as they stood shaking the water from their hair. Ianthe turned away to go and stretch herself in the sun, but, as I drew my breath for the plunge, I saw Marvan suddenly stiffen and gaze intently up at something on the high hillside. I followed her gaze. The sun was in my eyes, but I thought I caught sight of something slipping through the bracken, high up. It wasn't a sheep, because it had looked a lightish brown and smooth. A dog, or perhaps a fox? I wondered. Had Marvan and Ianthe not been both down in the glen I might have thought it could have been one of them. It might even have been Nuaman slipping along to surprise us. But I saw it only for a second. I looked at Marvan, but she dropped her eyes and turned away. She had sulked ever since Nuaman spoke to her before lunch, and now she marched away with her hands clasped over her round little behind and a toss of her hair as if she was offended.

When I came up from my plunge I looked round for Marvan, but she and Ianthe were already away up the hillside making for a broad flat rock about halfway up where we sometimes climbed to sit in the full beat of the sun. Katia was still hanging on to the bank, looking after the girls. I sent a fountain of water over her and she rounded on me and we splashed each other furiously for a few seconds. Poor Katia still had my scornful scepticism about Nuaman's tears on her mind.

"I tell, he *do* weep," she gasped when we both had a little breath again.

"Ertcha!" I replied and while she struggled for words I took a mean advantage and ducked her.

## 8

I had not been outside the Park once since I came to Ringstones. I had promised myself the day Sarkissian brought me in the trap across the moor from Blagill that one of the days—one of my 'days off' as I put it to myself then—I would go for a tramp across the moor. But I had not done. The Park seemed to suffice. Then, what need had I to go anywhere? Every few days Sarkissian would yoke out the pony-trap and go to Blagill, sometimes as far as Staineshead. He took the letters, brought the rations and did any other errands there were to do. The delight of Ringstones was that, as far as I could see, one could live there almost completely independent of the outer world. We had no electricity to be cut off, no telephone to go wrong and vex us. We reaped the benefit of the forethought of people who took isolation for granted: fallen trees of old Squire John Pococke's planting supplied Mrs. Sarkissian with fuel for her range, and the beck itself flowed through venerable lead pipes into our old-fashioned bathrooms. If candles and paraffin were hard to get it was light so long those summer evenings that we rarely needed them. The sun was our clock. The thrushes woke us and the bats told us when it was bedtime.

Mrs. Sarkissian put the idea of a picnic into my head. I had been saying that the sunny days seemed to be going on for ever. "Why don't you all go and take your tea out?" she said. "It'll be drier on the moor now than it has been for many a year, and you'd best go up there while it *is* dry!"

The suggestion fell in with something I had had at the back of my mind all the time I had been there. I wanted to go and see the Stone Circle. That evening I told Dr Ravelin that I thought of taking the children up on to the moor the next day. I thought we might go to the standing stones. As I said it I hoped that he wouldn't show that he saw the humour of the phrase 'taking the children'. He knew as well as I did by then that it was Nuaman who took me. To my surprise he said he would come himself. "It's time I got out into the sun and air a bit," he said when I protested that I did not want to take him away from his work. "Besides, that is my work, you know. I shall come and mingle instruction with your relaxation in the best Victorian manner."

Marvan and Ianthe, when I told them the next morning, seemed at first surprised, a little hesitant, and then, to *my* surprise, excited. I supposed that their hesitation sprang from their having been told not to go outside the Park by themselves.

"*May* we go...?" Ianthe asked with that inevitable glance round, looking for Nuaman's approval. Nuaman, however, was not with us at that moment.

"May? Of course we may!" I said breezily. "Dr Ravelin's coming too." It was then that their hesitation turned to excitement and as soon as we had finished the reading we were doing together they ran off to find Mrs. Sarkissian and arrange about the tea and sandwiches.

I met Nuaman as he came strolling up from the stables just before lunch. "Well," I said, "you're going to show me the Stone

Circle this afternoon. We're all going to take our tea up there."

He gave a quick little smile and shake of the head. Then, when I had explained clearly where we were going, I thought I saw a shade of discontent cross his face. It went immediately and then I thought, when he spoke, that I had taken for discontent what was really disappointment, for he said, pulling a rueful face: "Oh, I'm so sorry. I can't go. Sarkissian has promised to help me with something I am making and we have to do it this afternoon."

"Oh, Nuaman!" I said, disappointed, too. "Can't you put it off, whatever it is? Why do you want to stick yourself away in those dark old stables making things on a glorious day like this?"

He smiled and laid his hand caressingly on my arm and stroked it gently in the soothing, persuasive way he had which always did somehow persuade me and make me yield to him without feeling that I had lost the point. His hands were good hands: dry, cool and muscular and sensitive.

"Why," he said mildly, smiling up at me, "there will be another day. The sun will shine as long as I am here. I want it to!" And we both burst out laughing at the innocent and entirely convincing assurance he gave.

We were a party of five, then, who walked slowly up the narrow road on the Western side of the Park that afternoon; for Katia had got wind of the picnic, and with a brief and quite incomprehensible explanation and a vague gesture backwards, perhaps to indicate that the house could safely be left in Mrs. Sarkissian's charge for an hour or two, she picked up the tea basket and attached herself to us as we gathered on the terrace. She had put on an old dress, one that bore the stains of much romping and tumbling about the grass, but, as a concession to the sharp gravel of the road, she kept her shoes on. Marvan and Ianthe, in identical little linen frocks, walked as usual a few paces behind us, while Dr Ravelin, having offered to take the basket from Katia and been repulsed vigorously in Polish, or perhaps German, took the lead with me.

He halted us every so often on the road to point out with his ash stick spots of interest in the Park below. In particular, from near the top of the drive, he had us stand and gaze to make out what he was pleased to fancy the ancient bank of the road leading up from the Park. By dint of closing first one eye and then the other, or alternatively by half closing them both, I did succeed in seeing some kind of faint lines or ridges on the rough grass slope, which I was willing to accept, on his assurance, as the remains of the embankment of the ancient causeway. What was much plainer to me, because I knew it so well, was the circular unplanted track round the Park. From our position on the hill it was quite clear that it was designed and had not just happened so by chance.

When we reached the moor Dr Ravelin's keenness redoubled with the difficulty of his task. For there, try as hard as I might, I could not make out, across the billows of heather and the natural dips and rises of the moor, the traces of the broad way which he declared had led in ancient times direct from the top of the causeway to the Stone Circle. True, here and there a grey old stone did hump its back above the green, brown and purple sea, but it needed far more faith or training than I possessed to build out of those such a stately avenue of monoliths as Dr Ravelin wanted me to see. And then, I don't think I wanted to picture it like that; I liked the moor better for its wildness. Yet when we reached the low flat hillock on which the Stone Circle stands, I think that even without Dr Ravelin's guidance I should have been impressed by the recognition of human traces in a place where human beings seemed so out of place. As we came up out of the waist-deep heather on to that crown of smooth sward from which nothing of the Park is visible we stood still. The two girls and Katia slipped off their shoes, invited I suppose by the pleasant turf, but for an instant it seemed like a gesture of reverence; I almost looked to see Dr Ravelin put off the shoes from his feet.

Instead, using his stick as a teacher's pointer, he began very briskly to lecture on the plan of the area. I listened with only half my attention. For one thing, I was watching Marvan and Ianthe. Far from showing any reverence they seemed to have gone mad as soon as we got inside the Stone Circle, and while I followed Dr Ravelin sedately on his tour of the ancient monument they were capering about, dancing on the fallen stones, calling and shrieking to each other and generally behaving like chimpanzees in church. For the rest, I don't think I had any real interest in Dr Ravelin's information about dimensions, dates, orientations and comparisons with this and the other stone circle in places I had never heard of. I was content to saunter along with him over that deep, soft turf and drink in the still, brooding beauty of the place, its drowsy warmth of sunlit but soft greens and browns, the ancient stones, their hardness mantled with moss and a gold lace of lichen, dreaming there as though to idle through eternity in the sunlight; the rich blue sky above us, the scent of wild thyme and sun-warmed peat, and the faint summer song of insects.

But Katia was a practical girl. She began spreading out the tea, and chose for a table the very stone, a smaller, horizontal one at the bottom of the horseshoe formed by the standing monoliths, about which Dr Ravelin was just then discoursing.

"Not here, please," he said, smiling and removing the basket to the ground. "Archaeologists have been accused by sentimental persons of having no reverence for the bones of the heathen. Let us at least redeem our reputation by sparing the Altar Stone the desecration of our bakelite and buns."

Katia's eyes were just blue blanks of incomprehension, but after an appealing look at me in vain, she hitched up her dress and squatted cross-legged on the turf, inviting us with a sweep of her hand to range ourselves within reach of the eatables.

Dr Ravelin talked as we ate. "You see," he remarked when we had settled ourselves with our backs to the Altar Stone, "that the next horizontal stone before us—that one beyond the gap in the circle—the Sun Stone as it is called—is exactly in line with the lowest point in the Eastern ridge there. On June twenty-first the sun is first seen exactly in the centre of that dip in the hill. We have no true horizon here, so the altar is oriented on the apparent point of sunrise on Midsummer day. That is the argument for the heliacal character of the rites for which the circle was set up. So, it is supposed, some comparative limits in time for the construction of the circle can be inferred. The sun does not begin to reign over mythology until a fairly late stage in human history: until kings and warrior castes are firmly established in the direction of affairs. If that argument is sound surely the children of the sun never carried their golden legend into a stranger place than this. Except in such a rare summer as this, all about here is a cloudy wilderness of shadows: you would say the edge of the dark underworld of Hades rather than a bright arena of the sun."

I lay leaning on my elbow, enjoying the blaze of the sun on my body and looking through half-closed lids at the golden-skinned girls to whom, in the bright simplicity of their white dresses, that phrase 'children of the sun' seemed so appropriately to apply.

"Perhaps," I said, "they brought the sun with them, like Nuaman. He says the sun shines for him. Perhaps it really would shine for people who worshipped it. I feel I could worship it myself on such a day."

"Undoubtedly they brought him," said Dr Ravelin. "That is to say, they brought his worship. But why should the importers or inheritors of an elaborate solar cult pitch on such an unlikely place for their temple? Why should they go to the labour and expense of raising a stone circle here where it must be oriented on a sunrise which they knew was not the true sunrise? The answer must be a guess. Analogy helps. In Mecca that stone cube sacred to the heathen idols of Arabia became the holy house of Allah; in Cordova the moslem mosque became the Christian cathedral; in Lebanon I have seen in a niche in the foundations of a Greek temple a modern print of the Virgin; and I have seen a French-minted piastre-piece hung as a votive offering on a branch of a fig-tree by that fountain of Adonis which the people now call the River of Abraham. As new religion ousts the old it tenants the latter's temples. It is good strategy. A god turned out of doors commands little respect. But also, the conqueror sits on the vanquished's throne because it is a throne. The Lebanese peasant who climbs the rugged valley to make his offering to the Virgin at Artemis's shrine knows nothing about Artemis and not much about the Virgin; what he does know is that the place is holy. We cannot even guess much about who came here before these stones were raised but one thing we can guess: that it was a holy place before they planted these stones."

I listened lazily. "Somebody must have made it holy, I suppose," I said, "if *they* didn't." I wasn't at all clear who "they" were. "Hasn't anyone ever suggested that it was the fairies who made these places? This is exactly what I should imagine a fairies' dancing-floor to be like."

"Ah!" exclaimed the Doctor with a note of approval. "You

favour the older school of thought, do you? Elves, fairies, giants, magicians—certainly not just ordinary human beings must have raised these circles. That was the old belief. In Welsh legend there is an account of the origin of Stonehenge which attributes it to Aurelius Ambrosius, who may or may not be a legendary figure himself. Though there is evidence to suggest that Stonehenge was built at least two thousand years before Aurelius Ambrosius, yet the legend is interesting because it hints, in a poetical way, at something towards which archaeological discovery seems also to point. According to the legend, Aurelius Ambrosius ordered the magician Merlin to build him a stone circle on Salisbury Plain. Merlin, with a regard for economy which is entirely convincing, produced one out of stock. That is, by the power of incantation he removed one which already existed in Ireland and planted it down on Salisbury Plain. Now the interesting thing is that the legend also says that that same circle had been brought to Ireland by giants who carried it there out of Africa. Well, what is that but a way of saying that sun-worship and sun-temples were dimly remembered as an importation?"

"Still," I felt able to point out, "even though Merlin or some other magician had dumped this one down here, it doesn't explain why he chose this particular spot, which, you say, isn't lie right sort of place."

"No," said Dr Ravelin, "it doesn't. And there my theory seems to offer the only possible explanation. A church chooses to sit upon a heathen temple. Perhaps these ancient stones hold down something far more ancient, something far stranger than the men who placed them understood. Some queer feet have danced here, I feel."

"Queer?" I said, but I was not allowed to lie peacefully chatting with Dr Ravelin any longer. Marvan and Ianthe swooped down on me and hauled me off to play a game with them. I had brought a tennis ball along and, after considering the possibilities of the place, the four of us developed a kind of cross between rounders and tag: three of us scooting from base to base, for which the standing stones were very convenient, while the fourth tried to hit us with the ball. It was simple and satisfying. Marvan, Ianthe and Katia tore about like wild things and filled the place with such whooping and shrieking as, I'm sure, no convocation of Druids at a human sacrifice could have bettered. Dr Ravelin strolled away; the children's squeals must have been a little hard on his eardrums. We played until they looked exhausted and still I could not get them to stop and be quiet for a bit. Rut the game ended quite suddenly.

Marvan, who was 'it', had hurled the ball at Ianthe as she dashed for a base—it happened to be the Altar Stone. Marvan missed, and while she tore after the ball Ianthe jumped on to the stone and danced in triumph up and down, screaming derision after her. Suddenly, Nuaman stepped out from behind one of the standing stones at the back of Ianthe. He stood perfectly still for a moment, watching her. Then I suppose he must have spoken, for she whirled round and the moment she saw him she dropped off the stone and slunk towards him like a scolded puppy. Marvan, too, who had found the ball and was running shrieking back with it, stopped in her tracks and stood as silent as a fish.

I walked across. Nuaman, turning swiftly from Ianthe, gave me his quick, bright smile.

"Hallo!" I said. "What's the matter?"

"Oh, I changed my mind!" he cried gaily. "And then, I came up to find Katia. Mrs. Sarkissian wants her."

Katia clapped her hand to her brow.

"My goodness!" she exclaimed. "She say mustard make the supper hot!"

Before I had found a clue to what she meant she began bustling about collecting up the tea-things and I stooped to help her. I did not mind our game coming to an end: it was time to go, anyway. But that extraordinary change of atmosphere when Nuaman appeared puzzled me and annoyed me a little. And a more curious thing was, as I saw looking round from the tea-things, that Nuaman seemed to be speaking resentfully to Dr Ravelin who had come back into the circle. The Doctor shrugged his shoulders, took out his handkerchief, blew his nose, shrugged his shoulders again and seemed distinctly ill at ease. Then, walking over and clearing his throat, he said he thought he ought to be getting back to the house.

We all helped to gather up the things. The little awkwardness lasted only a minute or two and then Nuaman was as gay and friendly and the Doctor as much at ease as ever, and the girls in perfectly good spirits again, though well-behaved now.

Dr Ravelin had only part of my attention going back. Nuaman had as much to point out as he, but his were the things the Doctor did not see: a yellow pimpernel growing by a tiny trickle of water under the bank of the road, a stone-chat on the hillside, and the small speck of a kestrel hovering far away over the Park.

"You weren't in your workshop so long, after all," I said. "Have you finished your job? What is it?"

"Oh no," he said. "It's not finished yet. I shall have to work hard to get it ready."

"It has to be ready by a certain time, has it? Shall I be able to see it?"

I remember he had picked up a couple of pebbles and he clinked them together in his cupped hands as he glanced sideways up at me, gently teasing.

"Oh yes! You shall see it. Perhaps I'm making it for you."

"What can it be? Won't you tell me?"

"Ah no! You must wait till it's finished and ready for you."

"I see. It's to be a surprise, is it?"

"Yes, yes! That's it! A surprise!" And he threw his pebbles away and sprang laughing up the bank.

We waited at the front door for the two girls to come up. They had lingered behind us on the way down. They passed between us into the hall and it seemed to me that Ianthe gave me a significant look—a kind of 'I told you so' look—and made a little wry grimace. They went upstairs and Nuaman followed them.

Katia rolled her round eyes at me as she bore away the basket. "Too bad for all," she remarked. "Thank to goodness the Doctor there. Just so Ianthe become sorry. Become weeping."

"Well she's a silly little thing if she does," I said. Then, as I watched Katia go off to the kitchen, another interpretation occurred to me. I suppose it might have occurred to me before if I had bothered to study her particular misuses of English vowels. So that, I thought, turning a number of things over in my memory, is how Katia in the tangles of her own mind accounts for his cousins' obedience to Sir No Man!

# 9

I don't think I took my own guess at Katia's meaning very seriously; but still, I could not help teasing Nuaman when I saw him again the next day. It was the first cloudy day, I remember, that we had had since I came to Ringstones. I had thought of going swimming in the afternoon but the dullness of the day made me change my mind. Nuaman had not put in an appearance up to lunch time, so I decided that I would treat myself to a day's freedom and go to Staineshead. I had broken my watch-strap—one of those flexible metal affairs. I suppose I had strained it or loosened it while we were playing in the Stone Circle. My watch fell off in my room that evening and I found that the little flange that hooks the strap on to the watch was broken and the watch itself had stopped. Sarkissian was not going into the town for a day or two, it appeared, so I thought I might as well take the afternoon and evening off and walk across the moor to Staineshead myself. I studied the way on a map I found framed in the library. It seemed plain enough: merely a continuation of the track from Blagill. The whole distance from Blagill to Staineshead by this bridleway over the moor, I reckoned, was a little under seven miles.

I set out soon after lunch, estimating that it would not take me more than two hours to do the four miles, or two and a half if the track was not so good as the old map professed. I was nearly across the Park when I heard a hail and the sound of running feet, and turned to see Nuaman overtaking me.

"Well, Sir No Man," I said. "Where have you been all day?"

"I've only just got up," he confessed. "It was such a dull morning I thought I might just as well sleep."

"Ha! You see, the sun doesn't always shine when you want it to!"

He laughed. "No? But perhaps I didn't want it to today. I say, though, where are you going?"

"None of your business," I retorted, but seeing that he looked puzzled, I relented and told him I was going to Staineshead.

"Oh, but why?" he cried, as though going to Staineshead were a piece of wilful folly.

"Because I want to," I said. "I happen to have some business to do there. To get my watch-strap mended if you must know."

He glanced at my bare wrist. "But I can do that for you easily. You don't need to go to Staineshead. Give it to me. I'll do it today. I say, don't go to Staineshead! Come back and let's do something. I tell you what, I'll show you the old mine."

I had kept steadily on my way, and I shook my head firmly.

"No," I said. "I'm going because I choose to go, just the same as you chose *not* to come with us yesterday."

"Dear Daphne," he said, looking sideways at me with a kind of droll penitence. "I do believe you're vexed with me."

"Well, since you raise the subject, I must say that I wasn't very pleased with the way you behaved yesterday afternoon."

"Yesterday afternoon?" he repeated wonderingly, and then, gaily, "I say, wasn't Katia funny? I bet you never guessed what she meant when she said 'Mustard make the supper hot'."

"Katia's English defeats me," I said. "What did she mean? All I could think of was that we were going to have cold meat, but we didn't."

"No!" he shouted. "She meant musted. E-d, you know. The past tense of must. And she often says make hot for cook. She meant she had to go and make the supper cook."

"Lord!" I said. "I shall never learn Katia's language. I begin to doubt whether I ever understand a word she says. Do you know, she said something last night that made me think she was trying to tell me that you beat your cousins."

"Beat Marvan and Ianthe? Well, of course, I *do*," he said seriously.

I stopped. "What? You *do*?"

He looked at me blankly. "Why yes. You know I do. I beat them at everything."

"Really, Nuaman," I said. "You're almost as bad as Katia sometimes. No wonder you understand her so well. I don't mean that kind of beat. I mean whip."

He gave a hoot of laughter. "You mean like Sarkissian with the pony? Whip them to make them go faster? Shall I? Then perhaps they will beat me. Shall we put them in harness one day and see?"

I walked on again. "I almost believe you would if you had a cart to harness them to, and I believe they'd be daft enough to pull it. Katia would, anyway."

"I say," he said, grinning with mischief. "That's a better idea. You and Katia. I could make a chariot, you know. That would be fun! I'd be the chariot-driver and then you'd beat me because you'd be in front of me and I should beat you because I was behind you."

"Would you!" said I. "You'd have to get me in harness first, and that would be a bit more difficult than you think. But look here, are you coming all the way to Staineshead with me?"

"No. I'll just come up and show you the road if you must go, though I had much rather you didn't."

He sounded so wistful that I all but changed my mind. But I had taken it into my head to be obstinate, so I hardened my heart and carried on. He went with me as far as where the drive joins the track from Blagill. There, to my surprise, because I did not know he knew the district outside the Park, he gave me quite detailed directions about the path which, he said, was not easy to find.

I should have been glad of his company, but he was determined not to go, so we parted among the scattered stones in which Dr Ravelin sees his ancient ceremonial avenue. I turned right. The path was narrow, but quite distinct. No wheeled traffic goes that way now but shepherds and walkers must use it still. On the verge of a dip I looked back towards the fork and the Standing Stones. Nuaman was near where we had parted. He had perched himself cross-legged on one of the grey stones lying in the heather, a little, lonely, pixie-like figure in the wideness of the moor. Just before I turned with a wave to continue my way I saw, out of the tail of my eye, another little figure come up, as it were out of the deep heather, to join him; a little figure in brown and grey. The girls had been wearing their brown knitted silk jerseys and grey shorts that morning, but at that distance I could not tell which of them it was. When I came up the other side of the hollow and glanced back again both figures had disappeared.

As I remembered from the map, the path to Staineshead slants away gradually from Ringstones valley, bending in a westerly direction before it goes over Nither Edge and down into the Nither valley where Staineshead lies. I thought I ought to have been able to see the Edge, which was marked on the map as a crest or cliff, soon after getting out of sight of the Stone Circle. I suppose I had not taken into account that I was coming to it from the plateau and that it would look like a cliff only from the Nither valley below. I did not trouble much about looking out for the various marks Nuaman had described to me—a stone here and a tarn there; my path seemed fairly clear, and though I lost it a few times in boggy tracts of rushes where I had to make detours to keep my feet dry, I picked it up again on the drier ground where it wound among the heather.

I don't think I have ever been in such silence before. When I stopped to look round and there was no longer the scrunch or squelch of my own feet there was not a sound. The day was close and muggy; there was not a breath of air, and that, I thought, must be a rare thing on the moor. Not a curlew and not a single sheep called. I spoke aloud to myself once or twice, just for the companionship of my own voice, and I could not help wishing that Nuaman or the girls had come with me. I suppose that on a path that you don't know, in an unfenced stretch of country, with neither wall nor building, tree nor post to give you some idea of your progress, you are apt to be deluded about the distance you are traveling. After a time it seemed to me that I had done a good deal more than three miles and yet I had not come in sight of the edge of the moor where the land should drop down to the Nither. I am a fast walker, normally, but picking my way over that rough path and winding about for dry ways through the boggy places must have taken more time than I thought. It was, of course, simply because every bit of the moor looked so much like every other bit, and I knew it at the time, but I kept having the feeling when I saw some particular little pool in a hollow or a hillock with a stone or two on it that I had already passed that place before. I could almost fancy the last section of the path that I had covered sliding away and sneaking along behind a fold of the moor on one side to get in front of me and lay itself down ahead to drag out my way interminably. I kept glancing behind me, and I'm not sure that I didn't do so with half an idea that I might catch the path at its trick.

I don't usually mind being alone in the country. When I set out from the Hall I never gave a thought to the loneliness of the walk. When I was at home, at Whitehill, I often used to go for long walks by myself and never minded solitude. But I did feel lonely on Ringstones Moor. It wasn't "country" in that sense, at all. It was a strange, *private* sort of region. I felt that I was somewhere where I had no right to be, that I was trespassing. I wished that there was somebody with me to reassure me. It was absurd, because I knew the whole moor belonged to Dr Ravelin, and there was only the remotest likelihood of anybody but myself being on it, but I felt that at any moment I might be challenged. I began fervently to long for the sight of something other than heather and rough grass, brown peaty earth and yellowy-grey moss. I didn't like the wildness of the moor at all, now. I began to appreciate people's feelings about such places long ago when it was not good to be alone on a desolate heath. I remembered a place I had noticed on the map called 'Foul-Play Knowe'. The expanse all round me seemed quite empty, but it would have been difficult to see anything standing or crouching against the background of the heather.

At length I came to a long, gradual upward slope which, I thought with relief, must give me from its top the expected view down into the valley. I stumbled up it eagerly, but from the top I saw in front of me still a wide, hollow stretch of moorland, rising on its further side, which seemed to me in my disappointment and anxiety to be at least three miles away, to just such a long, heather-clad wave of ground as the one I was standing on. I suppose it was then that I admitted to myself that I had lost the way. I stood and looked all round. There was nothing at all that I could recognise. Away to my right, or a little behind me, I thought, should be the ridge of Blagill Moor, the Eastern ridge which we had seen so clearly from the Stone Circle the day before. But from this different position I could not recognise anything in the dim outline of the hill there, blurred as it was by the heavy, hanging clouds. On the opposite side my horizon was another line of dark grey hill, and before and behind me the brown sweep of the moor, very still and empty.

If there had been a gleam of sunshine I might have been able to decide roughly in what direction I was facing, but the clouds were a thick, uniform grey over all the sky. Perhaps, I

thought, I had taken one of the side-paths against which
Nuaman had warned me, and that now I ought to be heading for
the higher ground away on my left; perhaps the Nither valley in
reality lay beyond that. But I hesitated to leave my little path,
faint as it had become, and go ploughing through the waste of
heather and bog. So, after some anxious thought, I struck down
across the hollow in front.

I had not gone far when I came into a region of brown pools,
bare, spongy earth, stretches of greasy mud, and banks that
collapsed under my feet into holes full of green slime. I lost my
uncertain path entirely here, and in turning and twisting about,
trying to follow some sort of way along the necks of ground
between the pools, I lost all idea of my direction. Then I did what
I had been afraid of doing: I let myself become frightened of that
still, dead, slimy place. I let my imagination get the better of me,
and gave way to the thought that the place had deliberately
trapped me among its blind, dull pools and its hoary,
treacherous mosses. I felt its blackish-brown banks of peat
curling round me just as Nuaman had shown me one day the
sticky leaves of a butterwort slowly curling over a midge caught
in its glue. The moor frightened me. Its silence was not
mournful, but hostile. I began plunging and leaping wildly
across the pools and mosses with no idea but to get away from
that place.

It was a silly thing to do, for I mistimed some of my jumps
and I might well have landed in a pool that had no bottom. As
it was, I went over my knees at once and before I reached a
higher bank of dry ground and clutched the safety of the heather
roots I had been up to my waist and felt the suck of some
dreadful depth of ooze on my body. I lay for a short time in the
heather after I got out of that bog-hole; then, having pulled
myself together, I wrung out my frock and tried to clean myself
up a little. I even tried to whip up some spirit by reminding
myself of the joke of Mrs. Sarkissian's saying the moor would be
dry this summer. The infernal place would never be dry: it was
like a living body that secreted its own fluids.

Once away from that horrible still tract of bog I was more
annoyed with myself than scared. Why couldn't I have taken
better note of my bearings? Why couldn't I have paid more
attention to Nuaman's directions? Why hadn't I watched my

original path better? Tired though I had become, I drove myself vindictively forward across the stubborn, broken ground as a kind of punishment for my own stupidity.

I was quite lost. The only thing I could think of was something I had once read of in an adventure story: to find a stream and follow it down, no matter how hard the going. Thus, eventually, I should get off the moor down into some valley, and in a valley there would be fields, a wall, a path to guide me at last to a house or road. The thing to do, I told myself, as I recovered, bit by bit, from my annoyance with myself, was to take it steadily. It was impossible to be lost for very long or to come to any harm in England, provided no accident happened. I must not sprain an ankle, though, by stumbling among the roots or blundering down a bank. Provided I went steadily I was bound to find somewhere recognisable before nightfall, and even if I didn't I could sleep in a dry place in the heather and be none the worse for it. (I perhaps didn't sound very convincing to myself about this, feeling my frock wet up to the middle of my back.)

I made very toilsome progress, pushing my way through more than knee-deep heather and ling over frightfully uneven ground in the direction I had chosen, but, as if determination of itself can achieve results, I came suddenly to the lip of a deep, narrow valley in the bottom of which there rushed quite a big stream. I did my best to reason out where I could be. For all my weariness I could not have come so far from Ringstones. I might even have been making a great circle, as, I vaguely remember, people are said to do when they are lost in the Bush. Anyway, I thought, there could not well be more than one stream of this size within the distance from Ringstones Park that I could have come. This must, in fact, be the Ringstones beck, and I had come out on it somewhere well below the Park. If I followed it down it would bring me out into the Nither valley, but a long way from Staineshead, and I had lost a lot of time. I hated to have to go back and confess I had lost my way, but it was the only sensible thing to do. Besides, I was in no fit state to appear in the town. So I turned along the edge of the valley upstream, and soon found an easy sheep-track which led me along the slope, alternately over rough grass and through belts of tall bracken, below the level of the moor. I dared scarcely admit to myself what a relief it was to see bracken again instead of heather and moss and the bleached cotton-grass and the little dull orange spikes of bog asphodel, which I had almost come to look upon as a personal enemy by now. Then I saw a black-faced sheep. It might have been any sheep, anywhere, but it unreasonably convinced me that I was on familiar ground. My path grew broader and more assured. It led me round a jutting shoulder above a crag, and as I rounded that shoulder I had the strongest feeling that the view of the valley before me was familiar. The next crag, half a mile in front of me, which closed the glen to me from where I stood, must, I felt sure, be one of those two that stood like gate-towers at the end of Ringstones Park; and these thickets of birches below and the tufts of copse on the opposite side must be the ones I had glimpsed from the end of the Park itself. While there, beyond a little patch of level turf, screened by birch trees and thorns, was a dark opening between two slabs of rock; and that, surely, could only be the mouth of the ancient mine-shaft which both Dr Ravelin and Nuaman had described to me.

A moment later and I was quite certain, for among the birch trees I saw four or five human figures moving about. At least, my first momentary impression was that there were four or five of them, but then I saw I had been mistaken. Three figures came into plain view by the side of the beck and even at that distance I recognised the girls' brown jerseys, while the third figure, which seemed almost naked, though it had a glint of white about it, went leaping among the tumbled boulders at the water's edge in a way that would have betrayed Nuaman though he had been twice as far away.

He saw me and, while I made my way slowly along my high track, he crossed the stream and came slantwise up the steep slope to intercept me, running on all fours up the slippery grass as nimbly as a hare. He was wearing his white bathing trunks, the water still stood in droplets on his skin and his short dark curls were plastered to his head.

He took in my own bedraggled state with one long understanding look. He grinned, but I was so glad to see him that I forgave him his superior tone when he said:

"I knew you wouldn't find your way alone. Only Sarkissian and I can do that."

"Well," I said. "I found my way back. That's something!"

"Yes," he said, gravely, "but you must not go."

Without bothering about his clothes—or perhaps he had left them in the house—he led me up the glen, over the guardian crag and down into the Park. Never before had I trod its soft turf with such appreciation.

The girls were already back when we reached the house. I saw them hovering in the gallery in their white frocks. The way from the old mine along the waterside is probably shorter than the high path which we had taken, but, even so, I could not help wondering at the speed with which they had got home and changed.

"Now," said Nuaman, slyly, as we went upstairs, "you'll *have* to let me mend your watch strap."

"Dash it!" I said as I handed it to him, "I could almost believe you told me the wrong way just so that I shouldn't take the wretched thing to Staineshead instead of letting you have it!"

## 10

It was a very shamefaced account of my adventures that I gave Dr Ravelin that evening. After a bath I felt I felt little the worse for them, physically. My feet ached from stumbling in wet shoes over the heather roots, but I had escaped blisters. However, I suppose I must have spoken with some feeling about the mental impression the moor had made on me. Dr Ravelin looked at me curiously when I told him about my fright in that dreary tract of pools. He quoted something which I think was Greek, and then explained:

"Your sensations, you know, have been shared by other people in lonely places, and since buses and bicycles led people to give up using the path over to Staineshead, Ringstones Moor is a lonely place. I felt them once myself, long ago, in a desolate land, and I knew that that voice the pilot Thamus heard was a lying voice. Great Pan is not dead. He frequents his holy places still, and if we trespass there the fear of him falls upon us." "I thought Pan was a kindly god," I said. "But that place was evil. I was afraid of something."

"Why, so was Syrinx when she fled from Pan," said the Doctor. "That is the very duality of divinity. The god has always two aspects, one beneficent, one maleficent. Nor are they always distinct: the two aspects may be represented in the same act, or shall I say that every good act is doubled by an evil one, just as every gift of the fairies, who, by-the-by, might well be Pan's representatives on these moors, turns out to have some disastrous condition attached to it. Their gold, in the morning, is a stone, or their invitation to a night's revels holds the unfortunate mortal in a century's slavery."

"I think I should almost have been glad to meet a fairy this afternoon, for all that," I said, thinking of Nuaman sitting like a pixie on his stone.

"Well," said Dr Ravelin, quite gravely, "it would be interesting, but not surprising, if you had. The body of serious testimony to their frequenting this part is considerable. Though it is true, the last recorded encounters were not recent."

"You speak as if you took them seriously yourself," I said.

"Seriously? Yes, as seriously as I take any human belief which science tells us is erroneous but which yet has its significant monuments in literature or folklore or in stone. It has been argued, you know, that these little men, elves, pixies and gnomes of our great-grandfathers, are no other than the gods of our remoter ancestors; or, some suggest, an ancient people whom our ancestors displaced: the little metalmen of whom Olaus Magnus and Paracelsus speak; a shy population possessing arts unknown to the invaders, their memory still lingers round the earthworks and the stone circles which were thought to be of their building. Since people have ceased to see them the fairies have degenerated into vapid little wisps of things in books for children written, as it were, at second-hand. They have become the memories of memories. But once they were powerful and feared. So, should you meet one on the moor, Miss Hazel, be circumspect in your dealings with him!"

"All right, I will!" I said. "'Up the airy mountain, down the rushy glen'—I'll take Nuaman with me next time. I'm sure he'd be quite at home with little men."

I was not long in going to bed that night. On the way upstairs I looked into the housekeeper's room to say a word to Mrs. Sarkissian. She was sitting by the window, mending one of the girls' white linen frocks by the failing light. I said something sympathetic about mending and making do.

"Yes," she said. "Them two don't take no thought for their clothes. Look 'ere what Marvan done this afternoon." She showed me an impressive rent in the side of the frock.

"Some rip," I said. "But she couldn't have done that this afternoon. She was wearing her jersey and shorts."

Mrs. Sarkissian shook her head. "They was this morning," she said, "but they changed into their frocks soon as you'd gone, and Marvan done this on an old nail in the attic after tea. I only seen it when they came down for supper just afore you come in."

I suppose I was over-tired and my brain just would not function clearly, but, though I puzzled over what Mrs. Sarkissian said all the time I was undressing and while I snuggled drowsily down in bed, I could not make head or tail of it. But why it mattered whether they had been wearing their white frocks or brown jerseys that afternoon I could not quite decide.

This little problem, my tiredness and my panic of the afternoon all worked hard in my sub-conscious mind, no doubt, to produce the curious dream I had that night.

I dreamed that I woke in the middle of the night, aware of an unusual noise. I sat up and looked round the room. The clouds that had covered the sky all day had cleared away and it was moonlight. My window was open, the night was very still, and quite distinctly I could hear an irregular, metallic sound: ringing blows in quick succession, then a pause and a few isolated taps, then another quick tattoo, then another pause, and so on. The noise was quite inexplicable. I had heard nothing like it before at Ringstones. I got out of bed and listened at the open window. There, it seemed to me that the noise was coming from the back of the house. It was fainter and more distant, I thought, than if it had been anywhere close at hand in the Park. My bedroom door was open, and in the passage was a window that looked out at the back towards the old stables. I went out and listened at that window, and thought I heard the noise much more distinctly from there. It sounded exactly like someone hammering in the old stables. I don't know why in my dream I felt such curiosity to see what was producing the sounds, but as in dreams one sometimes seems to act with more decision than in waking, I went back to my room, put on my dressing-gown and slippers and crept quietly down to the back door which I opened very cautiously to avoid waking anyone else. I remember I did not feel in the least frightened.

Outside, in the black and silver of the night, I listened. The noise had ceased, but I had been so sure of where it came from that I went without hesitation down the path to the stables. I felt distinctly the chill of the night air through my thin dressing-gown, and the cold hardness of the flags through my slippers. I don't know of what my picture of the stable-yard was built up, for I had never been inside it in my waking life. I had seen its two big carriage doors from the outside and that was all. Now, it seemed to me, they were open a little way. I slipped through and found myself in a flagged court with stable and coach-house doors round three sides and a stone horse-trough in the centre. In the middle of the roof-ridge of the block of buildings facing the gates was what I believe is called in architecture a 'lantern', with a weather vane in the shape of a running fox, quite clearly to be seen in the moonlight. That, I suppose, I may have seen from the outside. One other thing I noticed which I could not have seen in reality was that the handle of the iron pump at one end of the horse-trough was finished off with a kind of flourished curl like a heraldic lion's tail, and the lead spout was in the form of a gaping lion's head.

As I stood looking round the clinking, hammering noise began again. At the far right-hand corner of the yard a pair of double doors stood open, the one towards me standing out into the yard so as to prevent my seeing into the place. A dim, smoky red light was coming from there and from there also came the noise. The moon cast an inky black shadow all along the right-hand side of the yard and I slipped up in the shadow and put my eye to the chink between the door and its jamb.

As in dreams one takes the queerest eccentricities of behaviour or dress as a matter of course, so I don't remember that I felt much surprise at what I saw, only an absorbing interest In the middle of the space inside the doors was an anvil; beyond it was a kind of blacksmith's forge from which the red glow came that lit the scene. With his back to me, stripped to the waist, and with his skin shining rosy in that light, stood Sarkissian wielding a hammer. Opposite him, entirely stripped,

as far as I could see, was Nuaman, his skin looking a rich gold
in the firelight, and he was striking with a smaller hammer.
Between them on the anvil was a curiously curved bar of shining
metal which was being held in place with a pair of long tongs by
an impish-looking little brown-skinned boy, crop-headed, sharp-
eared and as bare as Nuaman. At the forge was another couple
of naked brown boys, one pumping the bellows and the other
stirring something in the coals. I noticed the sweat glistening on
their skins. Sarkissian plied his heavy hammer and Nuaman
came down rapidly with his light one and between them they
were making that ringing, irregular music I had heard from my
room. They were working fast and concentrating with a fixity
that was truly dreamlike on what they were doing. What really
held my interest more than Sarkissian and Nuaman, or the
strange boys, however, was something that stood back a little
between the anvil and the forge, half in deep shadow, half in the
red glow of the fire, though at every stroke of the bellows the
glow brightened and leapt out to give me a glimpse of the other
half of the strange object. It was a kind of chariot, delicate,
elegant and shining with polished metal-work. It was a sort of
skeleton thing that looked extremely light and manoeuverable,
with the spokes of its wheels flashing and raying in the glow and
a red reflection leaping along its curving front rail. Its slender
pole sloped up away from me and I saw the end of it only by
snatches as the forge fire alternately glowed and dimmed. It
seemed to me that one side of the pole was furnished at the tip
with just such a curving bar or bow as Sarkissian and Nuaman
were forging at the anvil, and from this bar there dangled some
complicated kind of leather harness among which I clearly saw,
as the leaping brightness momentarily illuminated it, two
glinting metal rings, one of which, I was quite firmly convinced,
was my watch strap.

It was on this chariot that all the feeling in my dream was
concentrated. The litheness of its shining curves, the changing
light that seemed to give its sinuous shape a kind of breathing
life, the harness hanging empty at its bar, all had some sharp,
particular meaning for me. I knew it was an inanimate thing,
and at the same time I knew that it knew I was there. I was
terrified of it. It was waiting for me; and Nuaman and Sarkissian
were plying their hammers with demon-like haste to get it ready.

Sarkissian, Nuaman, the strange boys had not seen me, but it had. It winked and leered at me through the chink of the door.

I turned and ran on tiptoe out of the yard, back to the house, inside and up the stairs with the winged lightness of a nightmare. I threw off my dressing-gown and jumped, shivering, back into bed.

At my real awakening, which was in the brilliant light of a perfect morning, I remembered every detail of that scene and for a long time could not believe that I had not actually been up and out to the old stables in the night. I even felt my slippers to see if they were damp from the dew. Of course, they were quite dry. Indeed, I reflected, there wasn't much sense in feeling them, since if I had in fact taken the route I dreamed I had I should have been on flags all the way and should have touched no wet grass. Then as I sat on my bed pondering the thing, I was able to see from what different scattered incidents and ideas the whole picture was composed. The oddest thing now seemed to me something that in my dream had not surprised me at all: I mean the presence of the strange boys. I could see now that it was our talk of little men, of little metal-workers, the night before that had suggested them. Also, the puzzle over Marvan and Ianthe being dressed when I saw them near the old mine differently from what Mrs. Sarkissian said they must have been dressed at that hour, may have had something to do with it. I could see that my sub-conscious mind, dealing with the puzzle on which I had fallen asleep, might have suggested the explanation, quite reasonable when reason slept, that the brown figures I had seen in the glen were not Marvan and Ianthe at all.

The last piece of the puzzle fell into place even while I was sitting pondering it. I became aware of a tiny irregular ringing sound, just like that which I thought had wakened me in the night, but diminished now and all but drowned by the stir and noise of the day. My bedroom door was open; opposite it was the bathroom door, also open. I went across, and there I found the washbasin nearly full of water and a tap dripping into it with a clear, bell-like little noise. I must have put back the plug without thinking after I had washed the previous night, and when sufficient water had accumulated from the dripping tap, my sleeping ear had caught the sound magnified by the silence of the night.

## 11

I did not tell my dream to anyone. Having so satisfactorily analysed it for myself I shelved it. I had awakened with a head full of the detail of the queer scene and the strongest conviction of its reality but, of course, once I became busy with the realities of the day, this conviction deserted me and much of the detail slipped out of memory.

What occupied my mind more than my dream was where I had gone wrong in my way across the moor. During the course of the morning I went into the library to have another look at the map. There, sure enough, was a clearly marked bridle road from Blagill to Staineshead, passing within half a mile of Ringstones Hall. The Stone Circle itself was marked and also the private road down to the Hall. It seemed as plain as a pike-staff. True, the date of the map which I discovered after some search, showed that it was thirty years old. I must, I thought, ask Dr Ravelin if there wasn't a more modern one in the house.

As I was standing gazing at the map Katia wandered into the room with a duster in her hand. She seemed in unusually low spirits. I spoke cheerily to her and she came over and gazed mournfully at the map with me. I wondered what queer ideas it conveyed to her.

"Look," I said, jabbing my finger at the glass about halfway between the Stone Circle and Staineshead. "I lost myself there yesterday. Stupid, wasn't it?"

She looked at me as solemn as a ruminating cow for quite a long time, then nodded and heaved a deep sigh.

"I go one time," she said. "The road hide itself."

"It did more than that with me. It positively erased itself!"

Katia pondered deeply. I had not seen her look so lugubrious before, but I realised the hopelessness of trying to get at what was weighing on her spirits. It might have been a sharp word from Mrs. Sarkissian in the kitchen, or it might have been some profundity of Slavonic sorrow too deep for tears. I thought it might cheer her up if I proposed going swimming in the afternoon. She nodded, but still ruminated on something she seemed to want to tell me. At length, when she trusted herself to our slippery speech, it appeared that it was still my misadventure that she had on her mind.

"Sir No Man say no go," she said. "You go. He take the road away. I stay; you stay. If you not come perhaps I gone. Now both stay here one hundred year."

"Oh come, Katia," I said, understanding her mournful tone if not her words. "Don't you like Ringstones?"

She made her eyes very round.

"I like," she said. "I like to now. But now I *fear.*"

She laid her hand (duster and all) on my arm and, with her face close to mine, spoke the word with such heavily breathed emphasis that she alarmed me and for a second I had a most unpleasant feeling in my inwards and knees.

"Fear?" I repeated, noticing how the mere speaking of that word in a certain way can communicate the thing itself. "What do you fear?"

She looked all round the room, even took a pace towards the door, wavered uncertainly, then put her back against the wall and, looking as if she expected goodness knows what horror to burst in on us, pronounced in a whisper a word, or two words, that completely baffled me.

"Less she", or perhaps "Lest she", I thought she said.

At that very second the door softly and suddenly opened. We were behind it. It seemed to me, such was the state Katia's mysterious behaviour had got me into, that the door opened of itself. My heart thumped.

It was Doctor Ravelin. He did not notice us until he was half-way across the room. Katia fled; and I, having returned his absent-minded 'Good-morning' a little jumpily, turned again to the map, though I don't know that just then I saw anything that was on it. Dr. Ravelin had come to get a book from the tall case by the window. When he had taken it down we stood and chatted. Or he chatted; I listened for a few moments and then blurted out that Katia seemed to be acting very oddly. What was wrong with her?

He jerked his head up.

"Wrong? Wrong? How do you mean, wrong?"

"I mean," I said, his sharpness making me feel rather uncomfortable, "I mean, she says she's afraid of something."

He gave me a very long stare which seemed to cover a good

deal of thought, for at length he smiled as if he had understood the whole thing, and, moving away towards the window, he asked, "Did she say what she was afraid of?"

I told him what the strange word she had used sounded like to me. It seemed to puzzle him, for he knitted his brows and stared hard out of the window, but I suppose he was tracking it down in his own mind, for he suddenly laughed.

"Oh, *lies-schi*" (that's as near as I can come to the way he said it) "that's what she must have said." His face lit up and he leaned comfortably against the bookcase to explain. "Lies-schi are the demons of the forest. To Katia any wild place like our own moor here is a forest, and she's afraid that if you go wandering by yourself over the moor the lies-schi, or, as we might say, the goblins will get you. She's firmly convinced that they nearly got her one day when she missed her way when she was up there gathering bilberries. It's very interesting to me, of course. I find Katia quite believes in a legend that is current in different forms in many parts of Eastern Europe. It is said that there is a demon lord of the forest, an Elf-King, who roams with his band of goblin huntsmen through wild and solitary places, and should they find a mortal there, especially if it be a young girl, straying to gather kindling or mushrooms, they seize her and carry her off to their goblin kingdom, which they say, exists all the time in the forest where the Elf-King roams, but mortal eyes can't see it. These legends, you know, always foresee the objections of the literal-minded critic! Well, there the captive must make sport for the elves for the period of a complete year. They endow her with more than mortal beauty of form and face and she, together with others whom they have captured, spends all her time in dances and games for the entertainment of the Elf-King and his people. The goblin kingdom is all green lawns and glades of enchanting beauty under perpetual sunshine and the captive quite forgets her little hut in the village and the smoky fire and the drizzling sky. Then, when the very day of her capture comes round again she finds herself free and in the very place where she was taken. The forest looks just the same as it did, it is the same season, the same weather; but when she looks at her clothes they are falling off her with age, and when she holds up her hand it is withered. She was young a year ago, but now she is a wrinkled, hunchbacked hag. She hobbles back to the village and there she finds that during her one year's service with the elves a hundred mortal years have passed. Well, now," said the Doctor, taking breath and stroking the leather-bound volume he was holding. "It's most interesting to see the correspondences between this belief, which is still a living one for Katia, and some of our own fairy-stories. Take, for instance, the old Northumbrian superstition..." He caught my eye and checked himself, then gave a short, apologetic laugh. "Well, well. I mustn't mount my hobby-horse so early in the day! But if the Elf-King's pastimes interest you, dip into this work sometimes." He held the thick old book up for me to see the title. I read, in letters from which the gilt had long vanished, *The Secret Commonwealth*. The Doctor nodded, tucked the book under his arm, and marched to the door.

"By-the-by," he said, turning back to me with his hand on the knob. "It's most likely that I shall have to go away for a time very soon. I trust you won't mind staying here alone?"

"Alone?" I said, not quite understanding.

"I mean, of course, with the children."

"No, of course not," I said. I wondered, but could not well ask any questions.

We went swimming that afternoon: Katia, Marvan, Ianthe and I. The water in our pool was never warm. My swimming was usually a few minutes' energetic splashing and then a long lazing on the bank until I was hot enough to make another plunge into the chill bright stream desirable. Katia seemed not to feel the cold at all. Perhaps she had been inured to it as a child, breaking the ice to draw water from the mighty Bug or Og or some such river of the steppes. She was too dispirited to splash and play this afternoon. She stood up to her armpits in the middle of the pool, letting her hands float listlessly on the water and looking down in moony contemplation of her own body which gleamed distorted through the stream and pale against the dark brown rock beneath.

The two young girls, too, stood the cold water far better than I did. But they were always active enough to keep their blood well circulating. This day they were in a particularly mischievous mood. I tried to clear up the little mystery of what they had been wearing the afternoon before, but they chose to be pert and contrary. They answered 'yes' at random to my questions, then giggled and spluttered together over some private joke. They spent most of the time teasing and playing tricks on each other. Ianthe had taken it into her head to wear her gay little two-piece swimming costume, which she normally wore for anything but swimming. Marvan, as usual, was swimming nude. The distinction seemed to be an excruciatingly funny joke to her, and half the time, by sly approaches and sudden pounces, in the pool and out, she was trying to peel Ianthe's trunks off; but Ianthe defended them grimly.

"For heaven's sake," I expostulated, for the joke seemed to be one-sided, and I was getting a little tired of it, "why shouldn't she wear a costume if she wants to?"

Marvan chuckled. "She doesn't want. He says she must."

I gasped at the enormity of that fib—as Nuaman would have called it; but Marvan, snorting with laughter, swore again and again it was true, until Ianthe, seeing her opportunity, leaped on her and put an end to the matter for the time being by half drowning her.

As none of us had a watch we had to guess the time to go back for tea. Through such a long succession of sunny days I had learned to notice the shadows of the trees and to tell the time by them near enough for the way we lived at Ringstones. In the glen I guessed the hour, and when we got back into the park I saw from the position of the shadows of some of my well-known trees that I had guessed pretty accurately. I had just pointed this out to Katia, when it was confirmed by our meeting Sarkissian trudging along the drive away from the Hall with a pick and shovel on his shoulder. He had been doing some repair work on the road up to Ringstones Moor this last day or two and was now going up to do another spell after his tea. Little as I liked him, I admired his capacity for hard work; he was labouring at something all day long. I spoke to him as we passed and got a sort of dark leer in reply. Katia, who ought, I suppose, to have been home before us to get the tea ready, took to her heels and ran all the way back to the Hall.

I did not see Nuaman until late in the evening. The girls had had their supper and I had said good-night to them and gone out to stroll about the lawn in the middle of the park for a while before changing for dinner. Nuaman joined me there. I asked him how my "surprise" was coming on, for I believe he had spent the whole day in his workshop.

He shook his head and grinned. "Now, don't be impatient. It'll soon be ready."

"Well, what about my watch strap?" I asked. "Is that to wait until you've finished the other thing?"

"Ah, your watch strap," he said. "Do you know, it was so badly broken that I've had to make a new one. But I've made it just the same size, to clasp your wrist exactly. It won't come off again!"

We walked on until we came into the circular ride and there we turned and strolled slowly round the circuit of the park. He was in his sober, grown-up mood and for a long time said little, until, slipping his hand into mine, and squeezing my fingers hard with his remarkably strong ones, he asked:

"Do you want to leave Ringstones?"

We had not talked about my going away before. His asking that made me swiftly reckon up the time that remained to me and made me realise, sadly, that I had not so much longer to spend there. I hated to think of parting just then, and answered his question lightly, brushing the thought aside: "Oh, it'll be some time yet before I push off!"

"I want to keep you here for ever," he said, still gripping my hand hard.

"Ah well, you can't do that, you know. Everything has an end. Except a circle."

"A circle!" he exclaimed. "But Ringstones *is* a circle. And, look! We've made a complete circle now, and as soon as we've made this we begin another. You never can come to the end of Ringstones."

"Can't we?" said I. "We can, then. I'm going to make tracks across the diameter of this circle and go in and change."

He made no demur, and so we turned aside, through the trees and walked slowly, straight across the middle of the park towards the house. At the half-overgrown flat stone in the middle of the wide space of lawn Nuaman stopped and released my hand. It was the time of day when Ringstones was at its loveliest and when its dreaming peace and solitude seemed inviolable and everlasting. From that spot you saw and felt it most completely, for there the softly-coloured hills and the rich trees in all their heaviness of summer foliage made a complete circle round you. The house was hidden by a screen of copse. In all the visible world only the road on the hillside, seen here and there behind the rough vegetation that bordered it, told of this age and of human handiwork. I knew that I could never have enough of such loveliness, and that I should never in my life again know such profound content as that which Ringstones could give me on such a summer evening.

I think we were both reluctant to break the spell cast on us there by the evening light and by the unceasing song of birds and running water, powerful as an incantation to hold the mind in thralldom.

It was broken for us. Through that soft flood of music my ear caught a thread of harder sound: the distant crunching of wheels on gravel and the rapid clip-clop of a horse's hooves a long way off. Nuaman, whose ears were sharper than mine, had already heard it and was looking towards the slope of the Western hill. There, presently, beyond the trees of the park, the pony trap came into view with the pony going swiftly up the long slope of the road at its usual impatient trot. There was only one person in the trap, and that, I guessed rather than distinctly saw, was Dr Ravelin. We watched the trap until it reached the top of the road, and there, on the skyline, it pulled up and was immediately surrounded, as it seemed to me, by a number of figures, one tall one and a dozen or more shorter ones which came into view from further back on the moor. The sun was low over the hill and we were looking straight up into it. I was certain I saw the figures, but how they were dressed or who they were, I could not say. They were black shapes against the blinding golden light. Then, in a moment, the trap and they had disappeared over the skyline.

"So Dr Ravelin's gone. At this time of the evening," I said in wonder. "But who on earth were all those people up there?"

Nuaman looked at me, studying, I thought, my expression. But he spoke carelessly. "Oh that," he said, "that's Sarkissian, I suppose."

"Well, but the others?"

"Oh, the people who're helping him on the road."

He moved off slowly towards the house, thrusting his hands into his pockets and kicking the turf as he dragged his feet along, like any little boy pondering something important.

I went silently by his side. The deep sense of peace and harmony was gone. The friendly picture of the Ringstones I had grown to love had slipped aside and my first full view of the new one revealed where it had been left me with a weakness in all my limbs and a dreary emptiness in my heart. When Nuaman said good-night to me in the hall I could only stand and stare at his handsome, small brown face, so strangely vivacious, so complicated in its expression of triumph and delight, admiration, confidence and power. A wilder mischief than any I had seen danced in his eyes.

Half-way up the stairs he stopped, turned and leaned down just as he had done that first night; even then there was a caressing touch in his mockery.

"Good-night, dear Daphne," he said. "You shall see everything tomorrow."

Seeing that Dr Ravelin had gone, I told Mrs. Sarkissian not to bother to lay dinner in the big dining-room. I did not want to sit alone in the dusk. So I had supper with her and Katia in the housekeeper's room: a more cheerful place, but the company was little more cheerful than my own would have been. Katia was gloomier still than she had been in the morning. I think she had been weeping; and Mrs. Sarkissian would not talk about anything. Even to my direct question whether her husband had gone with Dr Ravelin, she replied only that she supposed so; and when I talked about the work-people on the road she was silent. She sat by the window with her head bent over her mending until it was nearly dark and I was forced to put down the magazine I had picked up to look at. Still, she would not light a candle. So we sat, all three of us, completely silent in the gloaming of the room.

Suddenly, making us all jump, the door was wrenched open. Katia leapt to her feet with a little gasp of fear, and I half rose, too, before I saw that it was only Sarkissian. I had not heard the trap return. Mrs. Sarkissian gave him a long stare, men bent again over the darning she could not possibly have seen. Sarkissian jerked his head back and Katia sidled out of the room, squeezing past him in the doorway with a cringing movement. Just as he closed the door behind the pair of them I thought— though it was too dark to be sure—I thought I saw him put his free hand on her shoulder.

## 12

I tossed and turned in my sleep. My mind worked furiously and yet I did not know what it was working on; images came crowding in on me, but I could not say images of what. I only knew that they were mischievous things that would not let me alone. It was too close. I threw my arms and legs about; something clung to my wrists and ankles. I squirmed and twisted to liberate myself, and at length got free of the clinging things and sat up.

The oblong of my window was faintly radiant with moonlight. I went over and looked out. The half-moon hung low in the West, over Ringstones Moor. I put my hand on the mullion of the window and the band of moonlight that fell across my wrist caught my eye. The moon held me by the wrist and something, I knew, was behind me. For a long moment I could not turn, and then with an effort I snatched my hand away from the stone and whirled round. The room was empty: my bed, my chair, my wardrobe and chest of drawers stood there, still and unchanged, only a little blurred in outline by the soft, uncertain light. I listened: there was no sound in all the house but the furtive, faint creaks of woodwork and little rustlings above the ceiling of my room. But I knew that I must move very quietly, for someone was awake not far away. I stood and thought exactly how I should dress myself and what I should take, then did it all deliberately and softly. I put on my corduroy slacks and dark green jersey and my walking shoes with rubber soles. I had a square, coloured silk scarf which I took from the drawer and spread out on the bed. On it I placed my powder-compact, my hair-brush and comb, a small first-aid outfit in a tin box which I kept on my dressing-table, my gym-shoes and my pocket French Dictionary. It was essential to take the dictionary, because otherwise the people where I was going would not understand me.

They did not speak French, of course, but with the dictionary I could make them understand. I folded the corners of the scarf over and tied them, making a neat bundle. Then very carefully, treading on the ends of the stairs near the wall so as not to make them creak, I crept down the stairs, across the hall and out on to the terrace.

Out in the open I was more alert and my hearing seemed keener that it had ever been. The night was warm and windless, but not silent. The night is never entirely silent at Ringstones. Little murmurings and movements of unknown creatures mingle with the endless soft gabbling of the running water. And tonight, or this very early morning, there was at the furthest range of my hearing a vague, whispering stir of some other activity. I had to be very wary. There was light enough to see the trees and the shapes of the hills distinctly; light enough to see anything that moved across the open grass. I ran on my toes over the milky white patches of moonlight and slipped, like a shadow myself, through the black shadows of the trees. When I reached the gateway in the wall that bounds the park, at the foot of the road up to Ringstones Moor, I stopped and searched under the trees until I found a thin stick. I knew what I ought to look like, because there was a picture of a Runaway in some bound volumes of the *Sunday at Home* which we used to have at Green Street when I was very little. So I slipped the end of the stick through my bundle and put it over my shoulder. Then I set off up the hill.

The road was very good. It had been widened, the holes had been filled in and the surface made smooth, and below it there was a neat grassy bank, like a sloping wall running all the way up to the brow of the hill. I went up the road quickly. I felt light and elated, but I knew I had to hurry, for, turning my head to the right I saw, beyond the indigo bulk of the other hill, a faint greyness creeping up into the sky, and I saw that the shine was fading from the face of the moon.

I reached the top of the hill where the road used to join the track from Blagill, and all at once my elation turned to such despair that I sat down on a stone and laid my bundle at my feet and wrung my hands. I had told myself all the way from the house that I must go to Blagill, not to Staineshead, and now I saw that there was no road to Blagill either. Sarkissian and the people who had been helping him had covered it over with earth and heather. Instead of the track to Blagill, there was a broad, smooth lane sweeping straight between the scattered stones of Dr Ravelin's ceremonial avenue up to the Stone Circle. The peaty soil had been levelled and reddish sand spread evenly over it. Nowhere among all the silvery greys and shadows of the wide moor was there any other road. The only way out of Ringstones Park led now to the Stone Circle. There, on their grassy platforms, sat the ancient monoliths: blind, still, patient things—blind, but keeping watch in the fading moonlight and the whitening dawn. I saw them grow paler and sharper against the dusky background of the moor. In the heather behind me a little bird raised the first voice of day, three tiny notes like drops of water tinkling into a bowl.

Then, as I expected, Sarkissian came up the road from the park. I could not run away because there was no road away from Ringstones. And in any case, I noticed now, without surprise, on each of the stones bordering the new-made avenue sat a little brown figure, cross-legged with its chin on its hands, watching me and waiting to see Sarkissian take me back. Their picks and shovels were leaning against the stones and they looked as if they were waiting to see something amusing after their labour. They were laughing at me because I had strode up so confidently to take the road they had hidden. Perhaps they would wait to watch me come up again, along their new road, after Nuaman had done something to me for running away. I was not in the least afraid of Sarkissian now; he could only do what Nuaman made him. Nor did he scowl at me. He looked amused. He wore no coat and his shirt was open to the waist so that I could see the jet-black curly hair on his breast When I stood up he looked down at me and wagged his head solemnly.

"You're a nice one, you are," he said. "Making me traipse all the way up here after you. I ought to have made sure of you last night with the other one."

Then he took out of his pocket something like a dog's lead with a very small collar attached, and this little strap he buckled tight round my left wrist. He kicked my bundle aside, but picked up my stick and switched it against his leg as he led me down the road. The light of dawn had washed away all the patterns of the moon when we reached the level park. I saw Sarkissian's profile very clearly as I walked along half a pace behind him. I saw the blue-black bristles of his cheek rooted in a skin that was blanched and deadened by the shadowless light of the early dawn. In his right ear there was a thick gold ear-ring which I had never noticed before. We did not follow the winding drive but walked over the grass, grey with dew, under the heavy-leaved trees where the birds were beginning those first songs which have such peculiar intensity and intimacy in the quiet early morning world not yet invaded by human beings.

"Are you taking me to the stables?" I asked.

He laughed ridiculously loud and long and kept jerking the lead and making my wrist jump while he laughed.

"You are a proper card, aren't you?" he said. "The stables! Ho, ho, ho, ho! You've a fancy to be yoked out, eh? Well, no man never drove a prettier pair. No, you're going to be put to school, Miss."

But we *were* going to the old stables. Although he led me by an unusual way through the tall shrubberies I knew that we must come out at the stables. The path was so narrow between the thick dark hollies and rhododendrons that I had to fall behind him; my rubber soles slid on the film of moss over the damp earth. Then we came out opposite the double gates of the stable-yard; and now a golden and rosy light was beginning to suffuse the whiteness of the dawn above the Eastern skyline and faint shadows were beginning to stretch away from the trees, across the grass.

We passed through the great gates which were open a little. Inside, everything was changed since the night I saw it before. The court was of vast width, paved with clean, creamy white stone flags. In the middle a marble fountain poured a rushing stream out of a gaping lion's mouth into a wide oval pool where the water wavered and winked, pale blue-green, while bands of light rippled below the marble rim.

All round the court were colonnades, and behind the polished cream and rosy columns were broad walks where people and chariots hurried up and down. On only two sides of the court were there now buildings: on the right was a long range of rooms closed with doors whose brazen hinges glinted against dark red wood, while on the side opposite the gates was a lofty hall into which I could see through arches opening into the long portico before it. It was filled with brilliant light from tall windows in its further wall, and there, among familiar apparatus, people were at exercise. I saw their figures bounding and flying past the open arches as they raced round after each other over the vaulting-horses, and I heard the rapid light beat of their feet on the floor and the crisp shouting of someone commanding them. The third side, to which Sarkissian led me, was a double row of columns through which, looking out in the direction where the Hall once was, I saw a far-stretching lawn, all spangled now with a diamond-sparkle of dew on a green and gold field.

Sarkissian halted and turned his head about, looking for someone. Out on the lawn bands of girls were exercising, and the people who jostled us as we stood were nearly all young girls like myself. Each group on the lawn was at a different exercise and each group was differently clad. Some, running, wore tight vests not reaching to their waists; some, being drilled in ranks, wore little white shirts tied with coloured girdles; others, naked, were wrestling in pairs; those in another group, throwing the javelin, wore just a slight harness of narrow white straps. In one place was a team of dancers, swaying and mingling in a mazy figure to a tune played by three little brown boys who pranced up and down piping before them; the dancers' sun-tanned torsos naked and gleaming above gauzy white skirts that swirled round them like foam among rocks. In another place was a group that glinted all bronze and silver: there, pairs of girls were fencing with short, broad swords and round shields on their arms; the bronze was the colour of their haunches and long thighs and the silver, a flashing piece of armour moulded like their own bodies to fit breast and back and ending in a curve at their waists. On their heads were shining, plumed helmets with visors to protect their faces. Plumes also tossed far away on the other side of the lawn where, against a dark-green wood, I saw the flash of turning spokes as the charioteers went back and forth, training their teams.

All were throwing themselves into their exercises with astonishing vigour and speed. None paused for an instant. The dancers wove in and out and the drilling teams shot out their limbs and bent and stretched as if their lives depended on it, and the fencers leapt back and forth and lunged and parried and the wrestlers struggled and writhed as if they dared not for a second stop. And all the time they were being urged on to more and more violent exertions by their instructors. These were all brown, prick-eared little fellows like those I had already seen:

impish creatures, no taller than Nuaman, but broad-chested, muscular, active and supple as cats. They wore broad white leather belts round their waists and carried short canes in their hands. Like little demons they darted everywhere, gesticulating, shrilling orders, cutting with their canes, stinging the athletes who dwarfed them into ever fiercer activity.

The colonnade itself was crowded as groups kept coming in panting from the field while others, hastily tying girdles or putting their harness straight, hurried out to take their places. Though I was dressed so differently from any girl there no one took any notice of me. There were so many of them and everything was going at such a speed that it was impossible to take note of all the varieties of costume and accoutrements or to follow all the different games and exercises, some of them strange and complicated, that were going on. It was an assembly of amazing grace and trained young strength; bodies freed for untrammelled action, displaying their taut beauty with confidence. On so much loveliness of form the light or shining dress some wore was a final touch of bravery, like blossom on a graceful tree. I was lost in envy and admiration and felt my will being overcome by an impulse, like that which sets the feet and body moving when dance music begins, to race out with one of those teams and fling my body fiercely into play, to strain and strive to my gasping utmost of physical effort under the wild urgence of one of those goblin commanders—those compact, brown bounding imps whose darting, shrilling fury kept all in fervid motion. But Sarkissian tugged at me.

Dodging in and out of the crowd in the colonnade were a few smaller girls who were taking no part in the exercise. They were slightly-built little things with dark hair and large, dark eyes, whereas most of the athletes were fair. These little girls, who were almost as brown as the boys themselves, were dressed in gaily-coloured little trunks and scarlet, orange or bright blue jerkins. They appeared to be acting as messengers or pages, running after the instructors. Sarkissian called to one of them. She came weaving her way through the people, and I saw that it was Marvan. Sarkissian threw the end of the leash by which he led me to her and left me and her there, waiting in the colonnade. Marvan drew me to the side of the lawn and looked up at me, laughing with friendly impudence.

"This is *our* school," she said. "It was very hard for us to behave properly when we were at yours." She wriggled and pulled a face. "Sometimes we didn't," she said.

The rim of the sun was now blazing above the Eastern hill and out there on the grass dresses and accoutrements were brilliant against the green. I could feel the promise of heat in the day. The group nearest to us, a team of sword-players, finished their exercise and came crowding into the colonnade, hot and breathless, with the perspiration glistening on all the bare skin their armour left exposed. Beneath the rims of their helmets wisps of hair stuck to their wet brows; their eyes danced and their cheeks glowed. Laughing, talking at the tops of their voices all at once, clanging their embossed shields, waving their plumes, jostling, pushing, slapping at each other with their blunt, wide swords, they blocked the colonnade all round us until their spry little instructor, skipping behind, drove them on in a compact knot with the last ones squealing and scrambling and trying to hold their shields behind them.

While I was still staring after them Marvan pulled me away. Sarkissian was beckoning to us from the court. I was taken to the farther side where a pair of high, bronze-studded doors opened upon the chariot house: an immense, well-lit place with a gallery running round the walls and a flight of stairs leading down just inside the doors. Here, pages and grooms were bustling about manoeuvring the graceful light vehicles, harnessing their teams of two, four or six girls or unyoking those who came perspiring in from the course. Up and down among them went the charioteers with their short-handled whips under their arms, bare except for little shiny cloaks flung back from their shoulders and gleaming white waist-belts bisecting their trim brown bodies. In front of them all, at the foot of the stairs leading up to the gallery, my own chariot had been wheeled out before a group of admiring onlookers. I recognised it by its shape and elegance. It was finished now; its polished metal and red and white leather-work were gleaming new and there was ornamental work in gold on its curving guard-rail. Each side of the bow-shaped bar at the end of its slender pole was furnished now with a pair of manacles of flexible metal. They had already brought out Katia. She was stripped, but wearing light, strong shoes, and her fair hair was confined in a golden net. Quickly, while she stood obediently in her place, the little men clasped the manacles round her wrists; her hands grasped the bar and they began to buckle round the upper part of her body the harness of white leather ornamented with gold which would hold her close yoked to the bar. Sarkissian appeared carrying another set of harness and gave me an impatient nod. Marvan undid the leash by which she held me and twitched my jersey.

I made no move. Then someone came running down the stairs and a well-known voice cried cheerfully:

"All ready?"

On the third step stood Nuaman, belted and cloaked like the other charioteers, except that round his head he wore a gold band in the front of which burned a great gem. Behind him, in an orange doublet, Ianthe peeped over his shoulder and grinned at me. Nuaman saw me and raised his brows. Then he laughed aloud.

"Come on! This is yours!" he cried.

He flung up his right arm and the movement made the thin black lash of the whip looped to his wrist writhe suddenly down the steps towards me. Still I did not move. Nuaman gazed at me, and before I dropped my eyes I saw his expression begin to change. The whole court, the whole school, had suddenly fallen silent; everyone seemed to lean a little towards me. Nuaman's arm drew back. I dared not look at his face, but I saw the lash wriggle back up the steps. Then, in the dead silence there came a rapid, loud grinding of iron-rimmed wheels on gravel and the plunging and trampling of a horse's hooves. I whirled round towards the great gates from which the noise had come and shouted with all the strength of my lungs, "Dr Ravelin!"

Before one of those tensely waiting figures could make a move I dashed across the court. I cleared the end of that oval pool with one bound and hurled myself through the opening of the gates into someone's arms.


The last line of Daphne Hazel's writing just filled the last line of the exercise book. I closed it, knocked out my pipe in the capacious brass bowl that Piers provides me with for an ash-tray, put out my light and rolled over to sleep.

# Part Two

# 1

I gave webs back the exercise book when we went up to his attic room again after breakfast. He took it and sat staring at the cover of it, frowning, not saying anything. It's always embarrassing to have to say something about an amateur's composition, and even though, in this case, it wasn't Piers's own, I did not want to hurt his feelings by dismissing the girl's story too casually. I erred on the side of caution.

"What I admire is the industry. The sheer hard labour of filling that book with writing is something that I feel would be beyond me at any rate. True, the thing is not finished, it seems: left in the air, rather. But still..."

"You don't think it's finished?" he looked up quickly.

"Well, I suppose the inference is: 'And then I woke up—with my toe fast in the bed-rail', or something like that. I suppose that's an acceptable end to a story. I don't know."

Piers nodded. "If it is a story," he said, but before I could ask him what he meant by that he added, "But doesn't anything strike you about the contents of the thing? The plot, if you like?"

We were approaching, I could see, the sort of discussion I wanted to avoid, so I took a side-track into something nearer my own territory, where I felt safer. The thing that had struck me, I told him, was the amount of browsing Daphne Hazel must have done among books of a sort which I shouldn't have thought would normally appeal to such a girl as I had imagined her to be. And, I said, hoping a man may be forgiven for hearing the buzzing of the bees in his own bonnet as somewhat louder than those in his neighbour's, I was curious to know where she got hold of that name for the boy.

"Couldn't she have invented that, if she invented the rest?"

"Well," I said, "she might have invented it, and by sheer coincidence dropped on a real, ancient Syrian name, but..."

Piers sat up, and, of course, needing little encouragement, I lectured briefly on the historical occurrences of the name and its probable application in ancient Syrian mythology to the same divinity who was also called Tammuz and whose memory—the point is irrelevant but interesting—is preserved in the modern Syrian and Hebrew names of the month July. More interesting, though perhaps equally irrelevant, I suggested, is the equivalence of Syrian Nu'man or Tammuz with the Greek Adonis, who is, again, the Eastern Adonai, the Lord, or King. A common flower in Mount Lebanon, if our Professor of Arabic is to be believed (which some have doubted) is the Red Anemone; and those flowers are known to the natives as 'Shaqa'iq un Nu'man', the sisters of Nu'man. Which, of course, is what Flecker was thinking of—

> *His father was Adonis,*
> *Who dwells away in Lebanon, in stony Lebanon,*
> *Where blooms his red anemone.*

Piers stared hard at the idea he chose for convenience to see written on my face for a long time, then: "She does make the point," he said, "that that wasn't his real name."

"Here," said I, "gimme the book again, I missed the Shaggy Dog somewhere."

He ignored my levity. "There's something about the pronunciation, isn't there?" he said.

I was pleased that he had spotted that. "Now, that is interesting to me," I said. "Somewhere your friend Miss Hazel has come across a remark about the peculiar difficulty any Christian larynx has in pronouncing the letter ''ain' which forms the second consonant of the name Nu'man. I was struck by her putting that in. I wonder what she's been reading? It sounds rather as though she's been dipping into an Arabic grammar somewhere. I begin to have a great respect for your friend."

Piers put the exercise book carefully on the table beside him and stood up. I was mystified by his manner. Daphne Hazel's excursion into fiction seemed to be worrying him out of all proportion. Then he began tapping his toe on the little iron fender round the hearthstone.

"That's it!" he exclaimed. "That is it! I couldn't have known that myself, because I don't know any Eastern language. I thought you might be able to see something there that I couldn't. Of course, she *heard* the name."

"Heard it? Instead of getting it out of a book? Well, she might have done. Come to think of it, if she'd got it out of a grammar she might have written the "ain' in a more scientific way. The grammars give lots of good advice about how to write it in English characters but none that's any use about how to pronounce it. But it's scarcely a point that you sensitive students of literature would consider important, is it? Fascinating as it may be to a pedant like myself."

"Of course it's important," he said, turning on me in some agitation. "Why should a girl like Daphne write all that and send it off to me without preface or explanation?"

"Well that," I replied, not able to help grinning, "is just the question I politely refrained from asking. I suppose we all have an itch to shine in something that's not our own metier. Your Daphne, who, I'll warrant, can creak a joint with any gymnast in the Kingdom, has a secret craving to cut as handsome a figure in print as she does on your wall-bars, your vaulting-horses, your parallel bars, beams, ropes and what else have you that takes the place of the racks and strappados of a less refined age. Why man, you scratch the same itch yourself. It's the right cacoethes, and time's the only D.D.T. I should simply say that her job at what's-its-name, this place, didn't give her enough to do. She was probably lonely, She amused herself by writing this, and as you're probably the most sympathetic person she knows, she sent it to you."

Piers shook his head. "I know her well enough," he said. "At school she never wrote anything—I mean, of that sort, imaginative. She can express herself well enough and she has read a lot. But, as I told you last night, inventing fairy stories is quite out of character in her. She just wouldn't have invented that story."

"Well she did. There it is. Unless she wrote it down from dictation or copied it from a book for some utterly unimaginable reason I don't see any other answer but that her imagination is capable of getting up to tricks that you never suspected. And, though I know little about the imagination and less about young women, it's not improbable that their fancies may fetch a frisk or two in private that you and I might never see but for some such whim as this."

"You don't see any other answer?"

"No, do you?"

"Yes. The answer I see is that this is not invented. It's a record of something that happened."

I expostulated. But my mind is less subtle than Piers's, or I haven't his practice in resolving ambiguities, allegories and the contradictions of actual and imaginative experience. I fear I did not altogether understand his argument that though the narration of incidents in Daphne's story might not, or could not, be a description of actual events which occurred, yet the experience dictating the form and character of the fancied events must have occurred; and, the choice of symbols in which to represent an experience depending intimately on the experience itself, the interpretation of the idlest fancies must reveal an active truth. Dimly I could see what might be troubling Piers, but the chimaeras he was tracking seemed to me to be denizens of a region of the mind too remote and mysterious for my plain conducted-tour kind of psychology to dream of venturing into. I can box the compass of sense with any man and do my bit of hawk-spotting between the cardinal points besides; but Piers was trying to make the needle point to a three hundred and sixty-first degree within the circle.

"Nay, Piers," I said in the end. "All these subtleties and hair-splittings, all these attempts to prove that black and white are interchangeable and that truth's only to be known by falsehood and cabbages to be recognised through a knowledge of kings, why, all this is but to say that if the lass has begun imagining things she never did before something has happened to make her."

"Well, I *am* saying that!" he cried.

"Why then," I said, "since it seems to prey on your mind, though I'm damned if I quite see why, there's only one thing to be done and that's to ask her why she wrote it."

"Good!" said Piers with quite an ominous note of satisfaction in his voice, and at once substituting action for argument he yanked a chair out of the way and reached down a bundle of Ordnance maps from the top of his cupboard. I began to commend the postal services, but protested with less and less vigour as he sorted out the right map and spread it out on the table.

"There, you see," he pointed out, "is Staineshead. We can go by train with a couple of changes, but I expect the bus is easier. We'll go down to the Haymarket and find out the times. Now, where's Ringstones? Ah! here it is. You see there's a footpath marked from Staineshead over Nither Edge, and a bridle road from Ringstones Hall to Blagill. And the Stone Circle is marked, too."

So it was. All as our author related: even to the loop of the beck round Ringstones Park and the Roman mine in the valley below.

"We'll go to Staineshead and then up the path to Ringstones," Piers said.

"And being much cleverer at that sort of thing than the heroine," I commented, "we shall not get lost. Nor shall I go up to my backside in a bog-hole. Oh no! Nothing like that. I've been over moors with you before. However, it's a jaunt, and if the wench is in jeopardy no Knight Errant, or erring, ought to boggle at a few marish wastes and deserts wild. Let me draw a dragon or two on the map just for the sake of appearances while you work out the distances between pubs. But," it occurred to me to point out, while he stared at the map like a hungry bloodhound at a bit of black-pudding in a porkshop window, "but do you know for a fact that this job of hers was at Ringstones Hall?"

"She says so," he replied, refusing to be drawn from the map. The point, however, seemed to me of some importance. Had she ever actually given the address of this place she was going to? In a letter, I meant, apart from the story in the book.

He lifted his head at last.

"Well, no," he said. "The last letter I had from her was from Towerton. She said the place was near Staineshead. That's all. Well, Ringstones Hall is near Staineshead."

I looked at those contours and that dotted line drawn with a confidence I have learned to mistrust in Ordnance maps and observed that if it was only twice as far as it looked I should count myself lucky. "Well, but," I persisted, after some aspersions on my map-reading which there is no point in repeating, "what about the book itself? The postmark?"

So we hunted until we found the brown paper it had been wrapped in. The post-mark would have defied a better epigraphist than I am. There was indeed a 't' in it, or something uncommon like a 't'. But so there is in Timbuctoo. I abandoned that line of enquiry.

"We can make a loop," said Piers, who had reverted to the map, "either by going on from Ringstones to Blagill or cutting across Blagill Moor, down on to the road, and back into Staineshead. We'll stay the night at a pub in Staineshead."

The last remark was made with quite unjustifiable assurance. Piers still believes, in spite of the weight of evidence from Joseph of Nazareth onwards, that an inn is a place where you can be put up merely for showing the colour of your money. However, Northern farmers are hospitable though landlords are surly, and, as the Highlander said in reference to the lack of another sort of accommodation, "Och, leddy, there's always the hill." It looked good country beyond Staineshead. The fine sunny weather was holding out astonishingly. I didn't think it mattered a damn whether we visited Daphne Hazel or not, but if Piers was so keen to see her I felt it was not beyond the powers of two able-bodied young men to discover the whereabouts of a Towerton girl, given a small place like Staineshead as a centre for the search. What sort of fools we looked when we found her was Piers's affair.

So we packed our rucksacks that evening and asked Mr. Debourg, with a firmness which I hoped I should feel the next morning also, to call us at five-thirty.


**2**


I tried to finish my night's rest in the bus, but it was a gesture—a bit of pitiful human defiance of the pitiless mechanical gods—and nothing more. It is perfectly logical, I suppose, that the more and bigger machines there are, the less room there is on this earth for human beings. But I do sometimes mildly wonder why it is that, although roads grow monthly wider and motor vehicles more enormous, though the adjectival noun 'luxury' is applied as a matter of course to the substantive 'coach', all the technical skill of the modern factory, backed presumably by centuries of experience in making things to measure for the human frame, has not succeeded in producing a bus where the leg-space is not one inch shorter than the average human femur and the seat space by just about the same amount too narrow to accommodate two average human pelvises placed side by side. Before Piers and I reached Staineshead the correct interpretation of the term 'luxury' had occurred to me. The adjective implies, of course, sumptuousness and opulence of appearance. Those tall-backed seats with curving lines, that wealth of plush and imitation leather, those chromium-plated knobs and ash-trays: such magnificence of upholstery, such generous filling of the available space with solid furnishings is indeed luxurious, but it has to be admired from the outside. A little further development and we shall have reached the point of perfection in buses; the point where the interstices into which passengers now insinuate themselves are no longer available to harbour such intruders but filled, they too, with luxurious appointments.

Piers, who was pondering other matters, did not treat these reflections very sympathetically. He ascribed them merely to my having been levered out of bed three hours before my usual time and promised me leg-stretching enough before the day was out. He paid just enough attention to my argument to demolish it by pointing out that if space, on my own showing was a valuable commodity to me, it was no less so to the bus company and we had as much of it as the price of our tickets entitled us to in these expensive times. Then he dismissed the subject for the more important one of Daphne Hazel's story.

All the same, he was as glad as I was to get out at Staineshead. I believe he had been there once before. At any rate, he wasted no time casting about for our way out but set off down the main street and across the bridge over the Nither and up a twisting lane or two to the edge of the town before he bothered to open the map. From that point, where we mounted a stone stile and took a path up a rough pasture towards Nither Edge, we had all the space we desired. I can never get among these hills of the North without their reaffirming my hold on an old conviction that space and silence are the most precious and least valued gifts left to us, in this crowded age, from the heritage of an ampler world. I mourn man's unhappy compulsion to fill them at all costs and with whatever rubbish comes handiest. I console myself with the reflection that, so far as the rape of space goes, it's but a late stage of a process that began with the first axe and the first plough. After the plough, the enclosures; after the wholesale conscription of open field and common to the cause of more economic exploitation, the ruthless trimming that pares away the lovely but uneconomic margins of our country lanes and roots out the extravagance of hedgerows. The rough and reedy pastures that slope up to Nither Edge, and the open moor beyond it still represent a bit of the old, casual, almost incidental way of exploiting land. As we climbed the wide and lonely hill, looking up to the tumbled battlements of dark grey boulders, aloof and hard against the summer sky, I greeted the freedom of the hill with something of reverence and compassion, as Caesar (one hopes) may have returned the salutation of those about to die. The next time I go that way, if ever I go again, I shall find Ringstones Moor turned into a plantation of pit-props or a tank training area.

We stopped to rest on the Edge, perching ourselves on one of the great rounded slabs of millstone grit with all the quiet Nither valley, a sober tartan of green fields intersected by black stone dykes, at our feet and the tangled, undulating brown, green and grey plain of the moor at our backs. Piers pored over the map. With his usual luck, which he calls skill, he had hit the right footpath out of Staineshead. It was evidently little used, and I thought little of our chances of being able to keep to it all the way across the moor to Ringstones. But there was not much fear of our getting lost. With a good map, a compass (which Piers usually carries with him on our expeditions) and a clear day, we might find ourselves toiling over some rough ground, but it was improbable that we should miss the Hall altogether.

As it happened, we lost the path a good many times, for it melted away every so often into a wide patch of heather or an expanse of quaking bog, and more than once eluded us in a maze of brown hillocks and holes. Some of these places were exceedingly difficult to get across dry-shod, and, as usual, after a time I got tired of tussock-jumping and just splodged through, with the inevitable result that soon I misjudged the depth of one spongy bit and went well over the knees into the bog. When I caught up with Piers I found him standing looking back at the tract we had just picked our way through. It was a broad depression in the moor, most of it bare of heather. Between the brown pools and pallid mosses the ground was naked peat, frosted, as it were, with some kind of salty exudation. Here and there a few bleached heather roots writhed up out of the peat like twisted skeleton hands. Even under a sunny sky it was one of the loneliest-looking bits of moor I have ever set eyes on. Piers remarked that this must be the place.

There was very little, it seemed to me, to identify it with any particular place—it was just a bit left over from the raw material of Creation. But then, recollecting that he was making the assumption that Daphne Hazel's story had some kind of truth, I saw what he meant I looked round and imagined myself alone there on a cloudy grey day. I should not have liked to be alone there. I wonder why we call a moor 'dreary'? It seems as little descriptive of the true character of such a region as calling a tiger 'undomesticated'. Dreariness is a human product. If I were looking for real dreariness I should go for a tour round the outskirts of Leeds or Manchester or Sheffield, where clinkery drabness falls with such a weight it would knock holes in the bottom of your soul. There's no comparison between that Waste Land and the lonely mountain. There is power in the emptiness of the hills; and it's a hostile power. One old tin-can lying on the ground would have made all the difference. But there was no tin-can: what we could see was all so powerfully un-human as to be able to erase our knowledge of its narrow limits. What existed was what we saw; and it was the same old menacing wilderness through which the Paleolithic hunter stumbled with backward glances at pursuing shadows—cold, hunger and death.

I agreed with Piers. It might well have been the very place where Daphne Hazel lost her way. I held my soaked trousers from my legs and conceded that I might well have found the very same bog-hole.

I noticed that Piers looked carefully about him on the ground as we moved on again; and once he stopped to stare at some faint marks on a patch of bare soil. I imagine he thought he had found a footprint; but Chingachgook and his son Uncas together, with Leatherstocking to help them, couldn't have said whether it was one or not. I told him so. Piers said nothing, and we carried on. We found the path again after a while; or at least a path. It seemed to run in the general direction that we wanted and so we followed it, winding and twisting through the heather over the waves of the moor. We came after some time to a little runlet of water flowing away to our left which must undoubtedly run into the Ringstones beck, and then, as we topped a low rise beyond this, Piers stopped and pointed. Less than half a mile ahead and somewhat to the right of our line of march was a round area, higher than the surrounding moor and plainly to be distinguished for being clothed with grass while all round it was heather; and, more conspicuous still, scattered about that green patch stood a number of great dark, upright stones. Piers studied the map and cast his eyes all round, checking our position. I complimented him on his navigation. There before us was the very Stone Circle indicated by gothic lettering on the Ordnance map.

We made straight for it, and soon we were sitting side by side on a large flat oblong stone lying within the circle. I pointed out the dip in the ridge which formed our Eastern horizon and remarked that Daphne's description was sufficiently accurate. Piers jumped up. "Yes," I agreed, "this must be the Altar Stone itself. But I shouldn't have any scruples about resting your hinder end on it. The sheep seem to have treated it with less delicacy than old man what's-his-name." I did my best to recall the description of the place in Daphne's story and, as I did so, recollected one particular that at once seemed to me to prove that she could not have seen the place with her own eyes. I mentioned it to Piers. But he thought I was referring to the clearing of the heather from the Stone Circle to the end of the Ringstones's private road. Of that, of course, there was no trace, and Piers began to explain again what he meant by imaginative and objective truth.

"No, no," said I. "I'm thinking only of the grass here in the circle. Doesn't she write that it was smooth and close-cropped? Well, it's as rough and tussocky as any old bit of moorland. I should say she had the description of the place from the old fellow who told her what it was like when he was a boy, perhaps, when the place was kept tidy."

Piers shook his head, and I don't know whether he thought my suggestion sensible or not. We strolled together to the edge of the circle on the side towards the hollow where Ringstones

Hall ought to lie. From there you scarcely perceived that there was a valley between the moor where the Stone Circle stands and the hill beyond. I noticed the bridle road from Blagill across the moor to our right, and saw where it dipped out of sight in front of us.

We picked our way across from the Stone Circle by a very faint and uncertain path, turned down the bridle road, which showed very little sign of use, and then, quite suddenly, saw the hill fall away before us to a steep-sided little valley. It was a surprising view: a deep cup in the moor, green and wooded; an open space of park-land in the middle and, towards the South-Eastern side, a stone house and outbuildings. We stopped and looked down. There seemed to be no one about. The only moving things were some cattle in the park.

"Well," I asked Piers, "what's your plan of campaign now we've got here?"

"Why," said he, "what's wrong with ringing the bell and asking to see Miss Hazel?"

"Nowt. Nowt at all," said I. "If we're lucky Dr Ravelin's old-world courtesy may extend to asking us to luncheon."

"It can hardly not extend to asking us in to see a friend, anyway," said Piers.

So down the hill we went. I quite forgot at the time to look out for the traces of Dr Ravelin's earthworks beside that rough, narrow lane. But as I remember the hillside now, so rough, so overgrown with bracken, ling and scrubby little thorn bushes and tufts of young birches, I doubt whether I could have succeeded in seeing any prehistoric embankment there though I had remembered and searched and stared all day. As we approached the level ground of the park it became obvious that Daphne Hazel had exercised to the full the artist's privilege of improving on nature. Like any new recruit to an order, perhaps, she had been quicker to learn its privileges than its duties. In the first place, the park was a good deal smaller than her story had led me to imagine; secondly, it was nothing like so trim and cared-for as I had pictured it. In fact, it was a sadly neglected little wilderness. Half the great trees were down, the shrubberies were scrub, the open lawns untended, rough with weeds and rushes and poached by the hooves of the red bullocks that turned their heads to follow us with slow stares as we passed.

Near the bottom of the hill a tumbledown stone dyke which had once, no doubt, been the park boundary wall was sketchily mended with posts and wire, which were also strung across the road to keep the cattle from straying. We straddled over and went across the park proper towards the house. Half-way across we set up a covey of partridges from the rough grass by the side of the drive.

Once down the hill you cannot see the Hall itself until you are almost upon it, the trees having been so planted and the drive so windingly traced as to give the impression that the park is bigger than it really is. Neither of us spoke as we drew near it. We were both busy looking about us, and I, for one, was busy also adjusting my mind to the new situation, both curious and comic, which dawning suspicions, derived from the observations I had already made about the place, told me we were going to meet in a few minutes. I don't know what Piers was thinking just then. From the intentness of his expression he might have been expecting Daphne Hazel to burst from the bushes at any moment with all the hounds of Elf-land in pursuit.

Then we came out, round a belt of beech trees, and stood before the terrace of the Hall. We stood there quite a long time. The first glance at the Hall was enough, but I continued looking at it because I dared not look at Piers. When at length I did, I had to sit down on the stump of a tree and let my sense of humour have its way. I've never seen such a picture of crestfallen bewilderment as he presented. But he saw the funny side of it himself after a while and sat down beside me and laughed.

It was Ringstones Hall, all right: I hadn't the slightest doubt about that. But the place hadn't been lived in for a generation. The chimney-pots were gone, many a slab had slid from the roof and the shutters hung rotting from their hinges in front of the windows; grass and weeds grew in the cracks of the steps and tall red docks lifted their heads as high as the ground-floor windowsills. The house was not quite a ruin, but it was in the last stage of dilapidation and decay; deserted, mournful, pitiful as only an abandoned house can look.

We went up the steps and across the terrace. The front door was half-open; it had sagged on its hinges and, by the accumulation of soil at its foot, many a long year had passed since it was last shut. We went inside, into a stone-flagged hall, and looked about us. Our entry disturbed a number of jackdaws in the upper storey and their loud alarm cries echoed hollowly through the house. We heard them fluttering and scrabbling about the roof and setting up an indignant clamour as they wheeled about the place outside. The entrance hall smelt of damp and mould. From the marks on the walls it looked as if they had once been panelled; now they were stripped and the bare stone was streaked by weather. Only the lowest stair remained. All the others, with supports and balusters too, had been ripped out, and the landing that hung inaccessible above was devoid of woodwork. We wandered into the other ground-floor rooms. All were alike, stripped and empty; doors, panelling, almost every scrap of woodwork gone; the plaster had fallen from the ceilings and the fireplaces were choked with twigs and rubbish.

It had been a good old house. We admired it even in its decay: a well-built place with room to move about With a little imaginative reconstruction you could see it as it might have been a century ago: a sober, dignified, solid place wearing an air of having been there a long, long time.

"Well, well, well," said Piers slowly when we came out on to the terrace again. "Let's go and have a look at the stables."

We went round the end of the house and pushed our way between two broad, high yew hedges which had once bounded a short drive but now nearly blocked it; then down a flagged path, all but grassed over, to a square of buildings in much the same state of neglect as the Hall. One side of the double carriage-gate was missing. We went through into the yard. Every flag of the pavement was outlined by a little hedge of grass and weeds and the stones themselves were green with moss. Piers walked over to a stone trough that stood in the middle of the yard. Beside it leaned an iron pump, red with rust. The spout of the pump was missing; the handle lay on the flags. It ended, I observed, in some sort of scroll ornament, half rusted away.

Most of the doorways round the yard gaped open. I wandered round and poked my head into a few of them. All were empty and smelt damply of long disuse. The roofs of some of the places had fallen in, but on the ridge of the block facing the gates there were still the remains of a wooden lantern with a bit of iron-work on the top of it which had once, perhaps, supported a weather vane. I paused in my tour of the yard at one corner to fill my pipe, looking idly into a bigger place with a double doorway which seemed to have been a coach-house. I stepped inside to strike a match, and, with half an eye, as I attended to the lighting of my tobacco, I noticed that the place still contained some mouldering vehicular rubbish leaning against the walls, while odds and ends of rotting leather harness and bits of old iron were strewn about the floor. There seemed to be some sort of wide old fireplace on one side. Piers, who had followed me and gone further into the place, poked about among the rubbish while the light of my match lasted.

"Two things at any rate," I said, as we walked back to the Hall again, "emerge from this reconnaissance. One is that we shall have to be content with our sandwiches for lunch, and the other is that we shall have to look elsewhere for your friend. Do you want to explore this place any more, or shall we have a shot at getting to Blagill before the pub shuts?"

He shook his head. He seemed quite satisfied, and in fact wore an air now of having expected the place to be like that. "There isn't a pub at Blagill," he said. "At least, there's none marked on the map."

He pulled the map out and thought for a time. I was a little puzzled by his manner then, but supposed that he was working out a new theory to account for Daphne Hazel's story in the fight of our discovery. I myself couldn't see what problem he could possibly find now in Daphne's bit of fiction, but, of course, we looked at the thing from different points of view.

"The quickest way back to Staineshead," he said, "would be to strike straight over this hill and drop down into the road on the other side. We could go to Blagill and trust to getting a bus, but I don't know how they run, and the main thing now is to find Daphne as soon as we can."

"Dammit," said I, "we're out for a walk. Not, mark you, that I don't think it would be quicker to stick to the footpath than to take one of your short cuts, but I'm not convinced of the urgency, anyway."

We crossed the park, Piers pointing out with rather a defensive air, as we approached the stream on the other side, that you could, with a little imagination, discern a kind of circular drive or track round the level space. We crossed the beck on the rocks and pushed through the marshy thickets of birch and willow on the other side, then tackled the steep hill.

Once we had got through the close and cobwebby plantations of conifers we stopped, sweating freely, beside a trickle of clear water and ate our sandwiches. After that it was a toilsome way up the moor. The sheep paths were not much use to us as they all ran horizontally, so we lugged ourselves slowly upwards through the tangle of bracken and heath, and finally reached the saddle in the ridge which we had seen from the Stone Circle. I say ridge, but it is a broad, more or less level mountain top, and, of course, most of it is bog and moss. It was very slow progress we made, but we kept advancing in a general Easterly direction, bearing, if anything, away to our left. It took us nearly as long to get over that hill as it had done to come from Staineshead to Ringstones by the path. But, of course, we couldn't have dreamed of going back by the same way we had come.

When, in the end, we got down on the other side and squelched in our sodden boots upon the metalled road we made up for lost time, and did a steady march of four miles an hour all the way to Staineshead. The bus from Blagill overtook us just as we came to the first houses of Staineshead.

Piers's idea was to go to the Post Office and begin his enquiries after Miss Hazel there. I agreed, but persuaded him to call at the principal pub in the place, the White Bear, and see if we could do something about our night's lodging. To my surprise, but not at all to his, they made no difficulty about giving us a room at a moderate price. We asked the landlady if she knew anything of Miss Hazel, but drew blank; however, she directed us to the Post Office.

I was wondering whether I dare propose to Piers that the investigation be postponed until we had had some tea, when our quest ended before it had well begun. Staineshead is not a big place, but still, the encounter was a stroke of luck. Half-way down the main street Piers suddenly exclaimed, "Hallo!" and darted off to the other side of the road. There, looking into a general store window, was a tall, fair-haired girl in a belted green frock, bare-headed, bare-armed, with a little boy holding one of her hands and industriously kicking out the toe of his shoe against stones of the shop-front.

Piers and the girl had already greeted one another before I came across to them, and were launched on half-embarrassed, half-laughing explanations, which were interrupted and made still more confused by my introduction, and then broken off altogether by our being joined by a middle-aged woman who came out of the shop accompanied by two olive-skinned, foreign-looking little girls of twelve and fourteen or so. We stood in a knot on the pavement and everybody talked at once, including the little boy, whose theme was simply and insistently tea. However, it emerged that the middle-aged lady was Mrs. Hancock, that she was Daphne's temporary employer, that little Bobby was her son and the two girls children of a friend staying with the Hancocks for the school holidays.

While Piers did most of the talking on our side, I, naturally, observed Daphne Hazel, the quarry, so to speak, of our wild-goose chase. She was very much the pleasant, active-looking girl I had pictured; just the girl who would have enjoyed such energetic gambols as she had described. Still, what struck me, and what couldn't well have been described in her first-person story, was her good looks. I admired in particular a most attractive combination of natural tones: a shining softness of pale hair, an intense blue of the eyes and a clarity of complexion where the blood brightened the light-brown tan of summer. That she recognised the satisfying harmony of those colours herself was indicated, I thought, by her having refrained from intruding on them any smear of synthetic carmine.

Mrs. Hancock made the amiable suggestion that we should go back with them for tea, so off we went on foot The house, it appeared, was not far out of the town. Piers and Daphne and the little boy walked in front and Mrs. Hancock and the two little girls and I followed on their heels. I was giving Mrs. Hancock a rather cautious account of our walk.

"Oh, Ringstones Hall!" she said. "Daphne and my husband can tell you a story about Ringstones Hall!"

I hesitated to ask what, because I was not sure how much she knew about Daphne's story, but then, from what Daphne was saying to Piers, I grasped that there wasn't much secret about it.

Daphne's voice expressed great surprise.

"But didn't you get my letter?"

"No," said Piers. "There was no letter."

"But I *wrote*," she protested, "and explained it all. I sent the letter off first, because I remember thinking when I was wrapping up the book, how silly—because I could have put the letter inside the book and saved twopence ha'penny. But I'd written the letter first and I licked the envelope and put the stamp on and gave it to Bobby to post without thinking."

She stopped suddenly and we all stopped. She looked at Bobby, a child, I suppose, of some nine or ten years, with consternation in her face.

"Bobby!" she cried. "You *did* post that letter I gave you on Monday, didn't you?"

The child, put on his guard and all his natural mistrust of adults roused by this concentration of attention, tried to divert it by skipping the direct question with a brief nod and immediately seeking to interest us in a project, of which he seemed to have information, to make the green Sheepcar buses extend their service to Staineshead. I sympathised with this gallant but hopeless attempt to create a diversion. A few more years would teach him that there's nothing so pertinacious as a woman intent on fixing responsibility for a lapse. Reluctantly, therefore, he abandoned the bus subject and admitted that he had posted the letter.

"Yes, but when?" Daphne persisted.

"Yesterday," came the sorry confession.

Daphne gasped, "Oh, *Bobby!*" and looked up at us, blushing with comical guilt.

"I forgot it on Monday, but I remembered it yesterday morning and I did post it all right," Bobby volunteered, finding explanation easier after an admission of the fact.

I don't think Piers wanted to catch my eye just then. The thought of the postman delivering the simple solution of all the mystery Piers had elaborated, probably at the very moment when he stood staring with a wild surmise at the mournful solitude of Ringstones Hall, was too much for me. My laughter puzzled Mrs. Hancock and it made Daphne's warm cheek glow the brighter.

"So *that's* why you came!" she said, as the full enormity of the misunderstanding sank in. "And you've been all that way to

Ringstones! Oh dear, what an ass I was. But I can explain it all...."

"I was just going to suggest that you might explain it over tea," said Mrs. Hancock, pleasantly. "Shall we go along?"


## 3


Mrs. Hancock's husband, she told me before we reached the house, was a doctor with his practice in Staineshead. The two young girls were the daughters of an Egyptian doctor, a friend of Dr. Hancock, who, it seems, had spent most of the war in Egypt. They were at school in England and had been spending the summer holiday with the Hancocks. Mrs. Hancock had thought it a good idea to get someone to come for the summer who could both help to look after the children and give them some tuition in English. It so happened that Dr Hancock had an old friend who was a lecturer at Towerton College and he had written to her on the chance that the job might interest one of the Towerton girls.

The Egyptian girls, Farida and Na'ima, were shy. They spoke English quite well, but only giggled when I spoke to them in Arabic. That, perhaps, is scarcely to be wondered at. I know only classical Arabic, which, I've no doubt, I speak with a Cambridge accent, and I have very little idea what barbarous corruptions may pass for Arabic in the mouths of present-day Egyptians. But here, at any rate, I thought, was another of Daphne's sources; and Na'ima's name solved the puzzle of the "'ain".

The Hancocks' house was a big one, with a spacious garden and a fine view of the moorland hills. Dr Hancock, who was waiting for us to begin tea, was a brisk, smart, jovial grey-haired little man, who could well have been the original of Daphne's Dr Ravelin. I was interested in his books, which filled many shelves round the big sitting-room where we had tea. He was not long in enquiring what we were reading at Cambridge, and soon he and I were well away on the subject of oriental languages. He seemed to have a fair command of colloquial Egyptian and some acquaintance with the written language. The little girls understood his Arabic all right and talked it back at him, and I'm afraid that in the interest of tracking down the classical origins of their dialect forms I rather forgot about Daphne's story. Incidentally, though, I had noticed that the doctor's library covered a pretty wide range, and among all sorts of scientific books there were a good few on anthropology and archaeology, including an abridged edition of *The Golden Bough* and several of Elliot Smith's and Perry's works.

Daphne did not begin to explain her story until the children had slipped away to play, and then she seemed to have such difficulty in beginning that Dr Hancock took the task on for her. He had laughed delightedly when he heard that we had actually gone to Ringstones Hall expecting to find her there.

"I know Ringstones well enough," he said. "I was born and brought up in this district. It was a fine old place once upon a time. My father was in practice in Neatsbridge when he was a young man and he used to go and visit at Ringstones. I've heard him tell how he used to drive up to Blagill and over the moor in his dog-cart to dine with old Dr Ravelin—he was a doctor of Divinity, not Medicine—and back again in the pitch-dark night, with a skin full of port-wine and a head full of tales about pixies and hobgoblins and ancient Britons and Romans and Picts and I don't know what. Old Ravelin was an antiquarian and a folklorist, and he and my father used to go at it hammer and tongs about the local legends which my father, being brought up on scientific principles, would try to find natural origins for, while old Ravelin, it seems, was all for the supernatural.

"That was before I was born. Even in those days a place like Ringstones cost a lot to maintain, and I suppose old Ravelin found it too much for his means. At any rate he shut the place up and went abroad and died abroad. It passed to his heir, a grand-nephew, I believe, who was in the Indian Army. Captain Wrightson, he was called. There was a family of Wrightsons at Neatsbridge. I used to stare at their memorial tablets in the Parish Church on Sundays when I was a boy. But they've all died out long since. This Captain Wrightson was not known here. Whether he ever came and looked at the old place I don't quite know. It's likely enough that he had the idea of settling at Ringstones when he retired from the Army, but that never came about. The house was left with a couple of caretakers in it, a man and his wife that Wrightson sent up from London, and George Iddenden's father at Blagill rented the park for grazing. Then Captain Wrightson was killed: broke his neck in a riding accident. I remember hearing of that. I suppose I should be nineteen or twenty at the time. It was not long before my father died. Captain Wrightson had no children. I suppose his executors must have tried to sell the place as it stood, but no one would buy so remote an old place as that. It's too isolated and inconvenient for anyone nowadays. I say nowadays, but it's thirty years since. Still, even then people wanted something a bit more modern than Ringstones! Bit by bit they sold what was saleable: the furniture and all the old panelling and woodwork, and in the end the Iddendens bought the place for the grazing land, and some shooting syndicate which has since gone bust bought the moor. Some of the stuff was bought up locally. That Koweit chest in the hall came from there, and we have a few other bits of things.

"Well, that was the state of the place when I began to practise here in Staineshead twenty years ago. There used to be quite a good footpath over the moor from here to Blagill, and sometimes I used to go for a walk that way and have a look at Ringstones."Daphne now chimed in:

"I'd heard all about Ringstones, you see, from Dr Hancock. It sounded an interesting place and I thought I should like to see it...."

"So we went," said Dr Hancock. He looked at Piers and me with an enquiring lift of his brows. "I suppose that's the adventure she told you about?"

Daphne looked at us all uncomfortably. "Well, no," she began, but Piers helped her out by asking the doctor to give us his version of their trip to Ringstones first. The doctor looked rather surprised, but then, quickly grasping that this was more complicated than he had thought, gave us a short and precise account of their walk.

"When was it?" he said. "About four weeks ago? Yes. My wife was taking the children off to her sister's in Sheepcar for the day. It was a Sunday. Daphne and I decided we would walk over the moor, have a look at Ringstones, and come back by the evening bus from Blagill. I hadn't been over for years before then, and I found that the path had got so overgrown that it was a hard job to follow it. In fact, though I couldn't very well admit it at the time, I got well and truly lost. On my native heath! However, I knew that if we only kept on long enough I should see something that I knew, and Daphne's a bonny walker, so, after some hard going over the heather and mosses, we did in the end sight the Standing Stones—the Ringstones, you know, that the place is called after. That was fine. No danger of going wrong from there; but, just as we were getting to them, Daphne put her foot in a hole and came an awful cropper. When I picked her up I found she'd sprained an ankle and cut her left wrist quite deeply by coming down with her hand among the stiff heather stalks. It was rather a fix. The day had turned very dull. I thought we were likely to have a thunderstorm. There's no shelter at all up there. Well, of course, you know that. There was no question of her being able to walk to Blagill with that ankle, and though, of course, I gallantly offered to carry her the remaining four miles, she made such objections to that that I didn't."

"Yes, I could see you carrying my nine stone all that way!" cried Daphne.

"Pooh!" said the little doctor. "I'd have tossed you over my shoulder like a roll of bedding. It was your dignity I was thinking about. Well, the only thing was to get Daphne down to the Hall, where she'd be sheltered a bit if it did rain, while I went off to Blagill to find some transport. I'm afraid we didn't improve the ankle getting down the hill, and it caused Daphne great pain. However, we got there. The door was open, I settled Daphne down on the bottom stair inside the front hall, got some water and bathed and bandaged her ankle and wrist with our handkerchiefs and then set off for Blagill as hard as I could go."

"Just fancy!" Mrs. Hancock appealed to us. "Leaving the poor girl all alone there in that lonely old place, miles from anywhere. And after all the tales you'd been telling her about the Polish girl, too."

"What had that to do with it?" demanded the doctor.

"Something, I think," said Piers, looking at Daphne, who, with brilliant eyes, was making the best of her embarrassment. "I should like to hear about her."

"All right," said Doctor Hancock. "As near as I can, I'll tell you. It happened while I was away in the Army..."

Mrs. Hancock interposed. "*I* can tell that story better than you. I was here at the time. Some people called Roebuck who live at Towngate End took on a Polish maid in the last year of the war. It's my belief that the girl wasn't all there. She used to drive poor Mrs. Roebuck to distraction; she never understood a word the girl said and the girl, I expect, never understood anything they said to her. She was a fine-looking girl as far as figure went, but I always thought there was something wandering in her eyes. Well, one afternoon she went out for a walk and didn't come back. She hadn't turned up by the time it was dark, and Mrs. Roebuck rang me up and asked me what she ought to do. She was imagining all sorts of things, except the obvious one which, to my mind, was that Katia—that was the girl's name—had hopped off to Nettleworth, where the Polish troops were then. Well, she kept ringing me up at intervals until midnight, getting more and more worried: she'd telephoned the Polish camp, and Katia wasn't there, she'd telephoned the hospital and she'd telephoned the police, and she couldn't hear a word of the lass. Finally, I persuaded her to leave it to the police sergeant here and go to bed.

"However, before eight o'clock the next morning she rings me up in great agitation and says she's had a phone call from the Iddendens at Blagill and they've found Katia. Would I take her over in the car to collect her. I was doing W.V.S. work then. So off we went, Mrs. Roebuck and I, to Blagill. There was Katia in the Iddendens' kitchen, looking as wild as a witch; old George grinning all over his face, young Joe looking very sheepish and young Joe's missus not looking at all pleased. Katia was wearing some of Mrs. Iddenden's things, and when we asked where her own were there was a certain amount of embarrassment. But young Joe told me the whole tale next time he came into Staineshead. It appears he'd gone up on his pony early that morning to look after some bullocks they had in Ringstones Park. On his way back he saw something white lying between those standing stones. Thinking it was a sheep that was sick, he rode over and then saw that it was a girl, stark naked, and, he said he thought at first, dead. But just as he came up, she sat up, gave one shriek and flew at him and clung to him for dear life. Poor Joe, he said all he could think of for a bit was that it was a good job there was nobody else about. However, he disentangled himself and gave her his coat and tried to tell her to stay there while he went and got his wife to bring her something to put on. But Katia wasn't having that He said she was terrified and he could make nothing of her, so, little as he liked the job, he put her on the pony and led her down to the farm and handed her over to his wife. He hadn't any idea who she was, but his wife, it seems, had heard that the Roebucks had a Polish maid, and as this seemed to be a foreigner she rang Mrs. Roebuck up.

"Well, of course, we tried to get out of Katia what had happened, but she'd lost whatever wits she ever had by then. She never had much English, and the most I could understand from her was that she'd met some people she called 'little men' and they'd played tricks on her and taken her clothes and kept her all night at the old Hall. She had obviously had a bad fright of some sort, but she didn't seem to have come to much bodily harm, except for a lot of bruises which, I suppose, she'd got through tumbling about the hillside in her birthday suit.

"The fact that she had been down to the Hall was proved when Joe Iddenden a day or two later turned up with her clothes. He'd found them somewhere among the old buildings belonging to the Hall. Katia, of course, was quite barmy. The Roebucks couldn't keep her and so they asked the Poles to collect her. But, bless my soul! they'd scarcely arranged with the Polish doctor at the camp to come and fetch her when off she flitted again. And this time they never did find her, though they got the police and the Home Guard and the Polish troops and the boy-scouts and everybody in three parishes scouring the moors for days. If she ever was found it wasn't in this neighbourhood, and nobody here has heard tell of her from that day to this."

"And, you know," broke in the doctor, hardly waiting for his wife to finish, "you wouldn't believe it in these days of popular science and the pictures, but somebody dropped a dark hint about the Duergar, and somebody else said, well, the Stone Circle always *had* been reckoned an uncanny place..."

"The Duergar?" we asked.

"Yes. I shouldn't have thought there was anybody left in Northumberland who knew the name outside a book. But it's odd how these things do linger underneath. The Duergar's supposed to be the wild man of the moors who hunts people down and carries them off underground. I haven't heard his name mentioned since I was so high and my grandmother used to tell me fairy-tales."

"Oh, that!" said Mrs. Hancock. "That's all a lot of silly nonsense. Somebody just said that for a joke. What I was meaning was that I shouldn't have been able to help thinking of that loony flitting about the place."

Piers wrinkled his brows. "And you'd heard about this before you went to Ringstones?" he asked Daphne.

"Yes," she said, "but I wasn't thinking about it particularly. I didn't much mind being left alone in the old Hall. It was broad daylight, after all. And my ankle was hurting far too much for me to worry about anything else."

"Yes, now, but let me finish the facts," said Dr Hancock. "I got down to Blagill, and by good luck I caught Joe Iddenden just as he was going out. I got him to yoke out the pony trap and come back with me at once. I suppose all told I was away from Daphne about two and a half hours. When Joe and I got back she was lying on the floor in a dead faint. I brought her round and we got her into the trap; but she was in a very distressed condition and I was puzzled, because the effect didn't seem altogether due to shock from the sprain, and there hadn't been all that loss of blood from the laceration of her wrist. Joe was very good. After I had given Daphne some treatment at his place he drove us all the way back here. I never thought about his adventure with the Polish girl then, but I'll bet he did! Daphne was a good deal better when we got home. We put her to bed, and apart from the sprain and a rather low temperature and slow pulse her condition was normal. By next morning she was quite well in herself. There now, those are the facts."

"I see," said Piers. "But you've missed out one, haven't you?"

"What?" asked Daphne, quickly.

"You had lost your watch, hadn't you?"

"Yes," she said. "That's perfectly true. The strap had broken. I put it in my coat pocket. They're shallow little pockets, and somewhere it must have fallen out. Perhaps when I fell down. I didn't miss it until Dr Hancock had left me, though."

"Well," I said, "but what did happen?"

I'm afraid this inquest was rather hard on Daphne. She looked very uncomfortable, and though she was obviously trying not to be self-conscious about it, I'm sure she was heartily wishing she had never obeyed the impulse to send that wretched exercise book to Piers.

"I don't really know how to explain this," she said, as much to Dr. and Mrs. Hancock as to Piers and me. "You know I amused myself while I had to stay indoors with this sprain by scribbling in an exercise book? I didn't show you what I'd written, because, well, it seemed such nonsense when it was written down. I just couldn't believe it myself, and yet I felt I simply had to write it all down. I suppose, having written it, I ought to have kept it to myself, but something—I really don't know what... I mean, like you do with a dream, I wanted to tell it; and Piers knows me, and so, on the spur of the moment I wrote a letter saying how I had come to write it, then parcelled the thing up and sent it off. I never dreamed, of course, that Bobby hadn't posted the letter. You must have wondered what on earth it was when you got the book without any explanation. But, I mean, how could I have imagined you'd go off to Ringstones to look for me?"

"Never mind," I said comfortingly. "We enjoyed it. I wouldn't have missed that bog-hole for worlds."

"If there is a bog-hole anywhere within reach you never do miss it," retorted Piers. "But still, what I should like to know is where you think the story came from. I mean, how did it happen in your mind? I must send it back so that you can read it," he said to the Hancocks, "if Daphne doesn't mind."

Daphne hesitated. "Well," she said frowning a little and scraping the crumbs on the cloth together with her finger, "well, it was a sort of dream, or a lot of dreams. I know that sounds impossible: I mean, one couldn't normally dream all that—all those conversations and so on. It's frightfully difficult to express this, but you yourself must have had a dream something like that at some time. I mean, one where you wake up and although you can only remember clearly one or two incidents, or one or two sentences that someone has said in your dream, yet you have the strongest feeling that there was a tremendous amount more that you just fail to remember, something that's there, and yet just eludes your grasp."

"The tail of the mouse disappearing down the hole," I said. "Yes, I've sometimes had that feeling after a dream."

"Well," she said, "this was like that, but somehow a much stronger feeling and such a vivid sense of reality that really, while I was writing it down, I did seem to be recollecting actual facts. As soon as I put pen to paper the whole thing came pouring back: I knew that all that talk of Dr Ravelin's that I'd dreamed must have been like that, and I knew I *must* have seen the park just like that, and that the girls and Nuaman must have done what they did do. I mean, I don't say that I remembered all that talk word for word, but I woke up with sentences perfectly clear in my mind and I knew that if so-and-so had been said then all the other must have led up to it."

I thought I understood what she was trying to say, and Piers supported her by telling us that once before his Tripos he had woken up in the morning convinced that he had composed a complete series of answers to a paper on Seventeenth Century Drama in his sleep.

The doctor was interested. "When did the dreams begin?" he asked Daphne.

"That's one of the funny things about it," she said. "I can't quite decide. I know that for a time after you left me in the hall there at Ringstones I didn't think about anything very much except the pain in my ankle and my wrist and how I was to get back; though, at the same time, I was worrying about my watch. It's only a cheap one, but I wish I hadn't lost it. Then I remember feeling cold, which was odd, because the day was close and sultry. I think I did get a bit frightened then. I began to feel that the place was awfully still and lonely, though there were faint little noises rustling about in some of the rooms, and quite suddenly, I remember, I heard some people, children they sounded like, laughing and calling to each other outside. I was absolutely convinced I heard them. I just couldn't catch the words, but they *were* voices. I wasn't frightened, simply because they were so real. I was thinking more of the shock they were going to get if they came inside and saw me sitting there at the foot of the stairs."

"The jackdaws," I suggested. "They can sound very human. They and the noise of the beck. I've once or twice been as convinced myself when we've been camping near a hill stream that someone was talking close by and had to get up to assure myself it was only the water."

"Yes," said Daphne doubtfully. "Yes, I suppose that must have been it. But then someone came down the stairs behind me and touched me at the back of the neck and then I fainted."

"What!" we all shouted together. "Down the stairs? There aren't any stairs!"

Daphne looked really startled. "Aren't there?" she asked incredulously. "But I sat on them. That's where you made me sit down while you bandaged my ankle, isn't it?" She turned to Dr Hancock.

The doctor looked at her very keenly. "You sat on the bottom step," he said. "But that's all there was to sit on. The rest of the stairs were taken out long ago. Didn't you notice when we went in? Well, no, perhaps you wouldn't. I suppose that ankle was giving you enough pain to distract your mind from your surroundings at that moment. That's rather an interesting example of the power of suggestion. You were sitting on a stair with your back to where the rest of the stairs ought to be, and even though you can perhaps feel that there's nothing behind you, yet your subconscious mind makes the assumption that the rest of the stairs are there. But I should say that in recalling what happened you have involuntarily transposed two events: you fainted first—the fatigue and shock could account for that—and after a partial recovery of consciousness there was this hallucination of hearing footsteps and being touched. There may even have been a slight delirium, though, at the time, the injury didn't seem to me sufficient. But you never know. I once saw a hefty Egyptian fellah pass clean out from a subcutaneous injection."

"You know," Daphne resumed, "I really did think that there were stairs there. I can't quite picture that hall without them. I can see now, I think, that all my dreams about the place were pieced together from what you'd told me before, not from what I actually saw there. I don't think I was quite conscious any of the time from that faint I did until waking up the next morning in bed here. At any rate, I have no clear idea at all of being put into the trap and brought back. Perhaps—I don't know—some disjointed land of impression of turning wheels and a whip cracking. But the next morning, although I woke up feeling all right except that my ankle hurt, I was absolutely certain that I had spent the whole time from that faint in one tremendous crowded dream and that, if I tried, I could recollect the whole of it in perfect detail, and, well, that conviction was so strong that I hobbled over to my chest of drawers and got out that new exercise book and my fountain pen and began to scribble it all down."

She sat back and looked round at us.

"*I* should like to see this production," said the doctor. "It's quite a feat to write down a dream, but it isn't by any means impossible. After all, reason and imagination step in to fill in the gaps between the genuinely recollected incidents of the dream. The neo-rosicrucians make a practice of it. I've seen some of their records of dreams. Astonishing farragos."

I nodded. I bad seen some too. It seems to me," I said, feeling rather pleased that my simple explanation of the story as an exercise in fiction had after all been a bit nearer the mark than Piers's mystery-mongering; "it seems to me that you had all the elements of the story, or dream, that you wrote already supplied to you here, from Dr Hancock's stories of Dr Ravelin's talks with his father, from the presence of these two little Egyptian girls and the little boy. Most of the matter of Dr Ravelin's archaeological ramblings might be dream reproductions of bits you had read in some of these books here, if you've dipped into them." (Daphne admitted she had.) "If pain can start you dreaming, and I suppose it might, perhaps underlying feelings of anxiety—I mean about your watch and getting home—might be expressed in a land of crazy story in which physical exertion and being held a prisoner were the main themes..."

Both Piers and the doctor opened their mouths and prepared to tear my theory of dreams to tatters, but I fended them off until I had got out something else that interested me in the story as a story.

"Half a tick before you Freudians charge," I said. "Just let me say that I think I can understand your dreaming all that—even the dream within the dream. I have a dim memory of double dreams myself. But there's one of your fancies I should like to know the origin of. This sort of gladiators' school: not that the general idea of that is strange. God knows, I still occasionally dream about the agonies of being chased round the gym at my own school. But I mean the chariots. I can see that it might be an expression of that feeling you sometimes have in a dream of being fastened to something you have to haul along—something that holds you back when you want to speed away; but I should like to know where you got the actual picture of girls drawing chariots. There's something I seem to remember in an Elizabethan play about pampered jades of Asia, and there's that prince of Thai Gin in Marco Polo who had his slave-girls draw him about his palace grounds in a little light vehicle made for the purpose; there is even a doubtfully authenticated story of the Indian Mutiny which relates that a son of the Moghul Emperor, when the mutineers took Delhi, had some of the English women captives stripped and harnessed to his carriage; but I wonder what you had been reading?"

Daphne grinned. "Well, I never heard that about the Indian Mutiny, and I'm ashamed to say I've never read Marco Polo. I do know the bit from 'Tamburlane,' but really, I can't think where I've read about those chariots. They were just there: quite a usual feature of the games. It was just that I felt that if once they got me strapped up to that pole..."

She rounded her shoulders and seemed to shrink from a present physical threat.

"Well," I said, "I suppose it just remains an unexplained quirk of the dreaming fancy, then. But still, the inspiration, so to speak, seems to me a bit inadequate. I saw that coachhouse place you mentioned, and I'm dashed if my subconscious, or imagination, or what-not, would ever have fabricated a gleaming chariot out of a few old bike wheels and bits of mouldy trap-harness."

Daphne began to object to something, but Piers interrupted her. "That reminds me!" he exclaimed. He fished something out of his jacket pocket and laid it on the table.

"That your watch?" he asked.

Daphne picked it up. "Yes. Yes. It is. But where did you find it?" I noticed again how extraordinarily brilliant her eyes became when she was excited; their blue light held my attention so as she stared at Piers that perhaps I was slow to understand why the warm colour of her brow and cheeks which had been so attractive a setting for the eyes' brilliance had now turned dull and cold.

The little doctor took the watch from her, wound it up, shook it and held it to his ear. He gave an exclamation of pleased surprise: "Well! *That's* none the worse, anyway. It's going!" He began to set it by the clock on the mantelpiece.

Daphne's eyes were still fixed on Piers. "Where did you find it?" she asked again, but her voice was almost a whisper.

"Why, in that coach-house in the stable-yard," said Piers, looking at her intently.

Dr Hancock jerked his head up. "Stable-yard!" he exclaimed. "You couldn't. Daphne never went near the stables. She couldn't have done. Could you?"

Daphne did not speak. I suddenly realised the cause of that peculiar brightness in her eyes, and I was shocked to see how far behind Piers I had been in understanding the depth of her distress. She held out both her hands, not to take the watch, but with a curious gesture of surrender as if offering the hands and wrists themselves to someone. I saw a newly-healed long cut on the inside of her left wrist plain against the sun-browned skin. She seemed to offer her wrists a moment and then, yielding to an unknown compulsion, reluctantly turned down her palms, curling her fingers round something invisible to us. No one spoke; I think we were all looking with a slowly rising fear at those two drooping hands, so helplessly waiting there. Then Piers bent swiftly across the table and seized both her hands in his, gripping them hard.

"Hold on," he said. "The watch ticks *our* time. The doctor did arrive in time, you know. He did arrive."

CPSIA information can be obtained
at www.ICGtesting.com
Printed in the USA
LVHW100252170123
737224LV00001B/199

9 781627 553605